SPINE-CHILLERS

SOMERSET & AVON

Edited by Lynsey Evans

First published in Great Britain in 2016 by:

 Young**Writers**

Remus House
Coltsfoot Drive
Peterborough
PE2 9BF
Telephone: 01733 890066
Website: www.youngwriters.co.uk
All Rights Reserved
Book Design by Ashley Janson
© Copyright Contributors 2016
SB ISBN 978-1-78624-129-0

Printed and bound in the UK by BookPrintingUK
Website: www.bookprintinguk.com

FOREWORD

Enter, Reader, if you dare...

For as long as there have been stories there have been ghost stories. Writers have been trying scare their readers for centuries using just the power of their imagination. For Young Writers' latest competition Spine-Chillers we asked students to come up with their own spooky tales, but with the tricky twist of using just 100 words!

They rose to the challenge magnificently and this resulting collection of haunting tales will certainly give you the creeps! From friendly ghosts and Halloween adventures to the gruesome and macabre, the young writers in this anthology showcase their creative writing talents.

Here at Young Writers our aim is to encourage creativity and to inspire a love of the written word, so it's great to get such an amazing response, with some absolutely fantastic stories. We will now choose the top 5 authors across the competition, who will each win a Kindle Fire.

I'd like to congratulate all the young authors in *Spine-Chillers - Somerset & Avon* - I hope this inspires them to continue with their creative writing. And who knows, maybe we'll be seeing their names alongside Stephen King on the best seller lists in the future...

Jenni Bannister

Editorial Manager

CONTENTS

VOYAGE LEARNING CAMPUS, BRISTOL

VOYAGE LEARNING CAMPUS - WESTON, OLDMIXON

WORLE COMMUNITY SCHOOL, WESTON-SUPER-MARE

THE MINI SAGAS

TICK, TOCK, TICK... TRAPPED!

One stormy night, a manor house stood towering over a miniature village. A poltergeist haunted the house. Turning over tables, slamming doors and rattling windows were its favourite games. A group of wandering travellers discovered the house and decided to stay the night. The precocious poltergeist took this as an advantage. Whilst they slept it commenced a night of mischief. It boldly flung a grandfather clock down the winding staircase. *Smash!* Rusty cogs spilt over the floor, crushing the innocent folk. Time stood still. The travellers forever trapped in their own haunted nightmare to spend eternity with their new friend...

AMELIA JAPPY (12)

THE WANDERER

With the terror of previous nights still haunting him, Charlie set out at first light. He saw an old man leaning on a rickety fence, his eyes vaguely familiar. However he was sure he had never met the man before. As he looked at him, the hair on the back of his neck stood up and an instant, cold sweat dripped down his forehead. The man's aura paralysed his body, his stare piercing his soul. Almost in a heartbeat, Charlie realised who the man was. 'You were in my nightmare!'

'I was indeed, and that nightmare is a reality... '

AMELIA MCGAUN BROWN (11)

I NEED A NEW LIGHTBULB

The light bulb flickered as he devoured the body. First he started on the still-beating heart. As his teeth sank deeply into it, ruby-red blood oozed everywhere, dripping down between the floorboards. He cracked a rib off the placid carcass, moving it in a steady motion in-between his barbed teeth. *Crunch!* The bone snapped, falling down his spindly throat. Chunks of tender flesh dangled from the boy's tiny hands. Blood gushed from the victim's colourless neck. He turned to me and gave me a devious little grin. His teeth freshly stained... Daddy had lost that tickle fight.

AMELIA CHAMBERS (13)

HEAT...

Why did I let them make me do this? Mother and Father think I am going to stay round Mellissa's house. Oh no, it's time. We are here at the asylum... Bits of wood cover the doors. We wait... Mellissa pushes me forward. I walk towards the door. There is an unwelcoming gap in the door. Sadly, I fit through perfectly. A china doll is on the burnt floor. A hand grabs me, pulls me down. 'No!' This house is going to be burnt.
'Stay with me.'
'Play with me Mother.'
The heat is overwhelming, fire is all around.

MAYA DAVIS (12)

THE DOLL

The kitchen was dull and blue. As Keira walked in, she felt suddenly depressed and wished she could leave the smelly house. Suddenly, she found the doll staring up at her with a grin on his face.

That night Keira woke, hearing footsteps coming up the wooden stairs. The door creaked open and the doll was standing there with Keira's food and drink for the morning. As she ate, the doll watched her with another grin. The doll left and Keira suddenly felt unwell, the doll came to check on her and her mum later. She was never seen again!

LAURIE MOWBRAY (11)

THE BUTTERFLY

Rosanna walked through the forest - butterfly ahead - twisting and turning between the hand-like branches of the trees. The moon was up, shining a path, guiding her way. She heard a rustling in the trees. *What's that?* she thought. She ignored it, following the butterfly deeper into the woods and further away from her family. Then the butterfly stopped. It fluttered to her hand. Rosanna looked at the thing of beauty. She started to feel dizzy; her vision started to blur. Suddenly, the butterfly sank its venomous black teeth into her hand. She collapsed to the ground. All went black.

RACHEL BAMFORD (13)
Bristol Cathedral Choir School, Bristol

UNTITLED

The peaceful lake was now black and boiling, twisting and contorting as a cacophony of screeches met my pained ears. Too soon, it became eerily calm. I stared at my reflection in the mirrored lugubrious waters. It became clearer; I could feel sweat plaster my face. My legs refused to respond. Time froze. My reflection smiled, its face morphed into an inhuman smirk. Steadily, it reached out of the water and seized my ankle, with a merciless grip I was hauled into the stagnant lagoon. The foul water engulfed and ingested me. The reflection smirked again. The world turned black…

GENEVIEVE KIERO-WATSON (15)
Bristol Cathedral Choir School, Bristol

WEREWOLF INVASION - PART ONE

One misty, gloomy, dark night at the stroke of midnight, a large group of teenagers appeared. But they weren't just an ordinary bunch. At night they turned into... Guess? Suddenly, a group of not just average teenagers appeared opposite the other group and the group turned into vampires! Also the other group turned into hairy, vicious werewolves. Both groups charged at each other as quickly as their legs could carry them. Then, *flash!* As they collided while hitting each other, a bright light teleported them through a black hole and into another dark, cold dimension. Forever!

CHRISTOPHER WOOD
Bucklers Mead Academy, Yeovil

THE HAUNTED HOUSE

I didn't know how long I'd been in the abandoned house, but one thing I did know is I wanted to get out. My teeth were chattering, my body shaking uncontrollably, I opened the door and saw the hallway; I tried to walk to the main door; it felt like the hallway was getting bigger and bigger, I began to feel dizzy. I swear I heard noises coming from the room behind me, I began to run as fast as my little legs could carry me. I got to the main door. I tried to open it, it was locked...

GEORGE LARK
Bucklers Mead Academy, Yeovil

NEVER FORGET

The old, abandoned, rickety house created a lopsided shadow on the pale green grass. It was crooked and broken. The only light on in the house was the attic window. The whole terrifying experience has made me shiver and tremble beyond belief. I definitely wouldn't sleep for a while, maybe ever!
I took a step backwards but tripped over a tree root. *Squeak!* The window opened. A cloaked head peered out. *Slam!* The window shut. The air filled with an evil cackle. It all happened so quickly. Too quickly. But I shall never forget that day. The day I died.

MEGAN WILLIAMS
Bucklers Mead Academy, Yeovil

GOD NEEDS YOU

Moonlight reflected off the cross on the front of the church. Inside, the vicar was packing his things to go. 'Where do you think you're going?' a loud voice bellowed behind him. The vicar quickly turned around, but nobody was there. The whole place didn't feel so holy anymore.

Suddenly staring into the eyes of a young man fear and anger swirled deeply in his eyes. The vicar felt a sharp pain in his lower abdomen. The mysterious young man had just shot him. As life vanished from the vicar, the young man bent down and whispered, 'God needs you... '

EMMA-MAE SEXTON (13)
Bucklers Mead Academy, Yeovil

DEAD SILENCE

'Where is Aaron?' Henry questions.

They go to Aaron's room and do not see him. They hear a groan. They see pale, dead eyes. Aaron lunges at them. They grab the nearest weapon (a crowbar) and *swing!* Matter covers the wall. They run out into the car to find Christina. They pull up.

'It's too late, she's a walker too.' The car speeds on. Stopped in their tracks, crowded by the dead, a roar of a chainsaw, 'Christina!'

'I thought you were dead!'

'Yeah!' Christina mumbles. A Bentley roars into life at Henry's parents'. No one is in. Dead silence...

HENRY WADHAM
Bucklers Mead Academy, Yeovil

CAMP

It was Friday night, 11:59. I was lying awake, I couldn't sleep. My friends, Charlie and Amelia were breathing deeply. I got out of my tent to go to the loo, when I came back, a bone-snapping sound came from behind me. I didn't dare turn to see what was waiting there. I turned, a huge creepy clown was smiling. I ran back to the tent as fast as my legs could carry me. When I got there I woke up Charlie and Amelia quickly. 'A clown is chasing me!' It burst in. We all screamed, 'Argh!'

AMBER C S WOODBURY (12)
Bucklers Mead Academy, Yeovil

HOUSE OF HORROR

One dark, stormy day, Sarah and Clair were walking in the woods. They came across a dark, spooky, abandoned house called the House of Horror.
As they approached, the door opened itself. Suddenly... a white hand pulled Clair into the dark house and that was all that Sarah saw. Sarah went inside the house, calling for Clair, but there was no answer. All of a sudden, the door slammed behind her and all that could be heard was the sound of two screams. They were never to be seen again. Nobody ever dared to enter, or ever came close either.

CHLOE BELLE BRITTEN (11)
Bucklers Mead Academy, Yeovil

Born Human, Living A Vampire

As I was strolling around my town, I started to feel a craving for blood. Only then did I realise who and what I was. A vampire! Troubled by my craving, I wandered back home, worried about my power and afraid of what I would do; I ran off.

I took refuge at the old, derelict church. I had become what I feared - a full-blooded vampire. The motionless body lay blood-ridden to my side in leaves. I knew what I had to do; I had to stay hidden and feast every now and again. That was it...

Luke Nother (11)
Bucklers Mead Academy, Yeovil

The Odd House

On this gloomy night there was misty fog. I strolled down the path. I gasped. In the corner of my eye I saw an eerie house. Floorboards were broken, the windows were shattered. I opened the gate... All of a sudden, a flicker, like a candle being blown out, lightning; as I walked up the gritty pathway I'd a feeling that my life was being sucked out! Darkness. Lights went off. I carried on; I got to the stairs. I took slow steps. It sounded like baby squeals. I was alone in the pitch-black; was this the end?

Jamie Bowles
Bucklers Mead Academy, Yeovil

THE RITUAL!

It was cold in the basement. It smelt of something that could poison your nose. As I crept down the squeaky stairs, there was an old wooden table which had an quill and an octopus head. There was a note! It said: 'Find the parts'. There was a map, X marked the spot. As I snatched the map, I sprinted up the stairs and slammed the door shut. As I turned the key I slammed my foot on the accelerator. I pulled up at this mysterious graveyard to find there was a shovel. As I started digging there was...

FRANKIE MERRITT (12)
Bucklers Mead Academy, Yeovil

THE HOSPITAL

Black hair, white, chalky eyes, a possessed ghostly figure, walking along dark halls of the West Lake Hospital. Through the children's ward, haunting each and every one of them. Making strange muttering noises, it wore a white, tattered hospital gown and a red band on skinny bone-like wrist. Stopping at an empty bed, it looked up at the board. A name was faintly written on it. Lucy. She was a lost soul, creeping around the ward, dragging a slightly ripped teddy bear behind her. A large, evil smile spread across her ghostly face. Be careful, she's coming for you!

ROBYN JACKSON (12)
Bucklers Mead Academy, Yeovil

The Abandoned House

The abandoned house really stuck out like a monster rampaging in a pet shop. It wasn't very pleasant. Sam was riding to school when he passed the abandoned house and he wondered, *what's inside?* Sam pondered how he'd get inside the creepy house. He grabbed a rock and smashed the window. Inside was empty except for a dusty, old music box. He went to pick it up, but he heard footsteps. He turned round, but it was too late... No one was sure what happened to Sam, no one ever dared to go inside. Sam was never seen again.

Adam Lock (11)
Bucklers Mead Academy, Yeovil

Circle Time!

8am, a good time to get up. Finally a break from school! The town had a rich history, I decided to look around. By 9:10am I was out the door. Curiosity got the better of me, I decided to go to the old school house.
As I went inside, I saw photos, these weren't happy children, there were no children. I looked over and saw doctors leaning over a patient, their legs were crippled. Stumbling back, I tripped over a box in the doorway, blacked out. When I came round, children circled around me. Help them, all but one!

Gina Walbridge
Bucklers Mead Academy, Yeovil

TRIP TO NIGHTMARE FOREST

Dear Diary,
Yesterday afternoon, I decided to take a walk to Nightmare Forest down the road. It was gloomy and dark outside, but then I entered the forest. The strong wind blew and the colossal, tall trees swayed. The ground started to shake and I heard some weird ghost-like sounds; they started silently and then got increasingly deafening. I was shivering, I felt a chill going down my spine. Other strange noises were starting to give me the creeps. There was something white hovering in front of me and it grabbed me and pulled me down...

NATASHA VICKERS (12)
Bucklers Mead Academy, Yeovil

THE HOUSE IN THE TREES

Jamie was walking down the lonely pathway when he heard a death-defying scream. Rain was hitting the ground ruthlessly. He was in an abandoned place looking for somewhere to eat his lunch. The rain was pouring through the leaves of the trees.
As Jamie walked down the slippery ground he saw a huge, old house standing right in front of him. All the windows were lit up... apart from one. Jamie felt an unusual tingle creep up his spine. He opened the rusty, brown door. *Bang!* It shut behind him, the room was swallowed by darkness.
'Welcome to my swamp!'

JAMES WHITFIELD (11)
Bucklers Mead Academy, Yeovil

DOOMED IN THE DARK

What happens if you have a *nightmare*, when you wake up, it comes *true*? You might not know, but I do.
It was nightfall, I went to bed.
I wish I hadn't.
The scene started off in a lurid forest, it was absolute darkness.
Behind me I heard rustling, I couldn't see, I heard more of them in front of me, around me, I was trapped.
I knew they were wolves, I heard them getting closer. They pounced at me, I saw them. Before they'd assassinate me, I woke. But I woke in the same, *dark forest*.
I was *doomed*.

KENNETH SETERRA (12)
Bucklers Mead Academy, Yeovil

UNKNOWN THREAT OF WILLMAN CASTLE

Rain scratched the cobbled walls of the castle, a car pulled up outside. A man stepped out and opened the door wide open, a grin on his face. He made his way down the torch-lit corridor, cobble walls cracked and clapped. He walked through an open door which led upstairs, a squeak of the wood cried out, each step louder than the other. A growl erupted from the door at the end of the hallway and the door flung open. He turned round and ran. The noises suddenly grew louder. His feet pounded on the ground like a bull's...

FREDDIE PAUL FRANKLIN (12)
Bucklers Mead Academy, Yeovil

THE GIRL IN THE WOODS

The rain was blowing in my pale face. Not being able to see, I was getting stuck in the squishy mud, tripping over the rustic roots of the trees. I don't know how I ended up here but I was scared, I wanted to go home. Suddenly, a beetle-black monster was coming towards me. What could I do? I gently stumbled backwards, not knowing where I was going. 'Who are you? What do you want?' The thunder getting heavier, I looked back, the monster had vanished. My heart pounded, I wanted to find my way out of this damp place...

STORM MITCHELL (12)
Bucklers Mead Academy, Yeovil

THE WHISPERING MURDERER

It felt like a normal day. I was walking home and somehow I ended up outside a house that I'd never been to before. I tried escaping but a strange whispering lured me back. The door opened to reveal a bloodstain on the floor. The door locked from the outside. The whispering started. I hadn't got any choice but to follow it. The whispering led to the basement. It smelt like fresh blood. There were people whispering. I couldn't tell what they were saying. My heart stopped when I heard 'murder'.
Then a child's worried voice whispered, 'Get out, hurry!'

LAUREN SMALE (12)
Bucklers Mead Academy, Yeovil

THAT LITTLE GIRL

It was a spooky night. A little girl was walking through a cemetery. She had black hair, skin as pale as a dead body and brown eyes. That girl had an old, white, torn-apart dress. She was walking forward with a sad face. Slowly, slowly, she approached two graves. 'Mum... Dad,' said a voice quieter than a mouse. The girl's eyes filled with tears. Then, at that time, a boy entered the cemetery. He spotted the girl and thought that she was lost. As he took a step forward, she started to disappear, never to be seen ever again.

PATRYCJA KACZANOWSKA (11)
Bucklers Mead Academy, Yeovil

THE APOCALYPSE

The rain fell heavy onto the graveyard. The thunder shook the ground, like the spirits were rising out the dirt. Maybe they were? A girl was walking through the graveyard. Lightning struck by her feet. The ground shook again as a green bruised hand suddenly shot up like a wilting flower, then more sprouted from the ground. The girl ran and hid in the church, locking the door behind her. She was trapped, terrified, she walked back and forth, thinking. *Bang!* They were in the church and then the apocalypse of the century started.

SUMMER SOPHIA LLOYD (11)
Bucklers Mead Academy, Yeovil

STOLEN SOUL!

I decided to go for a walk in the dark, shadowed woods. As I walked further into the gloomy woods, I heard wailing, distressing voices get louder and louder and then I saw it, the tall solid silhouette of the forgotten vampire boy from my dream. I stepped closer, only to see his red eyes and his pearly-white fangs snarling evilly. I decided to take a step back and run. The moss-invaded branches snapped below my feet and then I felt it pierce into my neck, quickly my soul was taken. I was one of them now.

CHARLIE RIDER (11)
Bucklers Mead Academy, Yeovil

THE MYSTERY MAN

On a blustery, snowy, cold winter's night, Hannah and Beth scrambled onto the bitter cable car, ready to go to the top of Washington Mountain. An ear-splitting screech erupted from the station as the car moved up the mountain. As they travelled up the snow-topped monster, Beth noticed a dark, hooded figure at the bottom of the mountain. The sisters were struck with paralysing fear. A tornado of questions blew through Hannah's mind. 'Bye-bye!' Beth let out a blood-curdling screech. 'Stop!' screamed Beth. The car detached and they fell. The man's plan was accomplished.

CONNOR STEPHENS (12)
Bucklers Mead Academy, Yeovil

Friday Night

I shuffled back into the kitchen, as I felt a spine-tickling chill coming from behind. The back door was wide open! The phone rang. A sinister voice came down the line... 'I can see you!' I slammed the phone down. A thud came from upstairs. I grabbed a knife and slowly crept up the stairs, all the lights in the hall were turned off except my bedroom. I ran next door to my lovely neighbour's house. Once I had told him what had happened he came back home with me. He went upstairs and never came back down again!

MOLLY ROUSELL (12)
Bucklers Mead Academy, Yeovil

The Maiden's Mansion

One day, a group of boys decided to take a short cut to school. The cemetery was always gloomy. One of the young boys was dared to spend one night in the mansion of the moonless cemetery. That night the boy returned to the mansion. As he took his first step inside he gulped. With fear as his enemy, he wandered the mansion. A shiver ran down his spine. The hair on the back of his neck stood up. He saw a maiden who kept bleeding where she had been decapitated! The ghost grabbed a knife. He fell, silently bleeding!

HOLLY LOUISE CUTTS (11)
Bucklers Mead Academy, Yeovil

Friday 13th July, The Sleepover Of Death

Dear Diary, Friday the 13th, it started there. We were trying to get to sleep but heard strange noises over the trees, sounding static. We looked out of the curtains and we saw a figure; we ran downstairs, outside and it was running away from us and we saw it disappear in a big green bush. We ran over to it, my friend peered in, it was an animatronic. It was purple, it had a bear's face, button eyes, Homer Simpson's stubble, it had a brown belly and looked like a killer. My friend screamed... I never heard him again...

Alfie Waddleton
Bucklers Mead Academy, Yeovil

The Chimney Dweller

Every night I'd hear crunching and snorting coming from my chimney. The soot would fall and leave a black mess on the floor. My parents said I was stupid but I knew what I'd heard. The days went by. I saw glimpses of the creature, all bony and black. It sounded like it was planning... 'Then she goes there, then dies!' I grabbed the phone and tried to call the police but the black creature emerged from the sooty chimney armed with a sharp knife. It smiled, throwing me in a corner and slicing the deadly knife through my neck.

Alice Church (12)
Bucklers Mead Academy, Yeovil

DEATH

An eerie silence hung over the forest draped in foggy darkness. Twigs broke beneath my feet as I moved slowly forward. In the corner of my eyes it moved! My balance was lost as I spun to face my worst nightmare... DEATH! An organisation that was fought off in 1982 but had somehow made a reappearance. It all made sense now, why members of my team had gone missing. DEATH was recruiting! I turned to run but a cold hand grasped my arm. A voice spoke; it was one I recognised. My last emotion was betrayal! My brother is DEATH.

LUCY GALE
Bucklers Mead Academy, Yeovil

TERROR IN THE FOREST!

Anything can happen there, especially when you can hear creepy noises, no one knows where they come from, maybe the forest? There were two teenagers and one kicked a ball into the bush and as David (one of the teenagers) went to get it a black figure approached him. David was pushing through the bushes, not knowing that the figure was following his footsteps. Suddenly he felt a quick push. 'Um!'
The figure looked like he was floating. David had no idea he was behind him. Suddenly, David felt some soft hands grabbing him on the shoulders. Why him?

LIAM SAMWAYS (11)
Bucklers Mead Academy, Yeovil

THE HUNT

My heart was pounding and my pace was quickening. Looking over my shoulder, I saw its blood-red eyes and pearly-white fangs, snarling. I carried on running, dodging the trees surrounding me, branches snapping beneath my feet. I raced from the horrifying beast. Ahead, I saw a clearing. Open space. I broke free from the forest into the heavy rain, cold drops trickled down my spine. There was no escape, no way out. My legs lost feeling. I dropped slowly to the ground; and there was the beast, teeth bared, towered over me, removing all life from my body.

ABIGAIL GOLD (12)
Bucklers Mead Academy, Yeovil

A WALK IN THE WOODS

Thunder banging, lightning struck, rain grew heavier when a petite girl crept through the horrifying wood. She was scared of what could be in there! Loads of people had been known for disappearing in the spooky woods!
She flinched as she heard a rustle in the bushes. 'Who's there?' she stammered with a chill in her spine. She saw a figure move! 'Who's there?' she shouted as she got a glimpse of the crooked smile of a... 'Ghost!' she screamed. She was paralysed. She tried to run but she couldn't. 'Argh!' she screamed.

LUCY CHATWIN (11)
Bucklers Mead Academy, Yeovil

No Escape

You're in a gloomy room with a flickering candle. 'What?' You see two doors, one leads- 'Hello?' to Heaven, another to Hell. 'Who are you?' Choose a door. 'OK... ' You pick the one to your right not knowing that Satan is waiting to pluck out your soul and devour your bones. 'Aw, Hell no!' You jump back, choose the door to your left... 'What the- ' Well, with the war, pollution and stuff too, many people died so it's too crowded... 'I'm breaking the walls down!' This isn't how it works! Uh, I can't be bothered with this anymore, goodbye!

ROBYN GRAHAM
Bucklers Mead Academy, Yeovil

Ghost

The fog settled on the town, making the air damp and cold. The grass felt freezing on my bare feet. I carried on walking calling out my dog's name, but my voice must have seemed like a whisper against the howling wind. My clothes clung to me. I called again. Wait... something was up ahead! A tall, glowing figure... maybe they'd seen Misty! I ran towards them. 'Hello... ?' They were gone! Where were they? 'Hello... ?' But my sentence never finished. As I fell down the cliff, the last thing I saw was the glowing figure peering down at me...

HANNAH-MARA MCGOWAN (12)
Bucklers Mead Academy, Yeovil

ABANDONED HOUSE

Fingers trembling I put my hand on the crippled oak fence. I vaulted it with caution... My feet squelched in the thick, wet mud and crows all around squawked in the eeriness. My body was shaking violently as if I couldn't move and I was paralysed. The shadow of the great, abandoned house loomed over me. Uncontrollably, I walked up to the doorstep and placed my pale, shaking hand on the door handle. I swung open the door. The hinges snapped and collapsed in a heap on the dirty floorboards. A moan came from the ceiling above. 'Help me! Help!'

CAMERON ROBERT DEY (12)
Bucklers Mead Academy, Yeovil

BACKWARDS

Every night I would escape to my hide, behind the mental hospital. One night, hunched up, I heard a noise - like someone asleep. I peeped behind the bush. A man laid there with long, greasy hair, yellow teeth; bloodshot eyes. 'Urgh!' he grunted, blinking at me. 'Who are you?' I asked, shocked.
'My name is Rellik,' he replied. With that, letters RELLIK appeared on his chest, written with blood.
Time passed. We crept back into the building, looking into a mirror. On his chest was the word: 'Killer'. He pulled out a dagger from his pocket and mouthed, 'You're dead!'

FAITH SCHOOLEY (11)
Bucklers Mead Academy, Yeovil

WHY ME?

Crash! The thunder roared. I tiptoed into the graveyard. The pale moon hung above, lighting up a tall gravestone. Realising, the date engraved was today. A howling noise arose in the dark. My blood turned cold, as a bulky, crouched figure appeared. It slowly crept towards me. I screamed as it lunged at me, a flash of lightning shot down. The monster's claws scratched my neck; blood ran all over. It aimed for my face. I kicked as much as I could. Just before I took my last breath, I looked at the gravestone. My name was printed on it...

SHANNON LAVERTY
Bucklers Mead Academy, Yeovil

DEEP BLACK MYSTERY

The lightning struck, the thunder bellowed and the rain grew heavier. It was 20:32. A little boy called Jimmy lived with his family. Jimmy was so tired that he'd soon fallen fast asleep.
In the middle of the night, Jimmy heard a high-pitched scream; ferociously leapt out of bed, to almost be paralysed. He ran cautiously to his parents' room, where he noticed they were gone! He raced down the stairs to a black hole gaping wide open. He'd collapsed in shock! His voice echoed away! Was he ever going to return? Was he even alive?

LAURA NICHOLSON (11)
Bucklers Mead Academy, Yeovil

THE NATIVE AMERICAN ECLIPSE

One day, a young native American boy asked his father, 'Why do we fear our first tribe leader?'

'Well, 2,000 years ago, a man named Adewatebenate created our tribe. He built a settlement and everyone respected him. One day he gathered 15 strong warriors and said, 'We'll attack the next tribe. Our colony must grow. This is the way it must happen.' The men disliked this, so at night, they stood in the forest and shouted, '2,000 years from now, we'll return and destroy this worthless tribe!' 2,000 years ago to this very day. Those men are going to return... '

JACK PAUL MILLS (11)
Bucklers Mead Academy, Yeovil

THE HOLLOWNESS OF STARS

There was no one to save her, to help her. A hollowness was inside her, spreading, growing, flourishing. It wasn't long now. It wasn't long before they had her. Had her in their slimy hands. In their twisted minds. She knew she wouldn't escape this time.

This would be the freshest air she breathed for the rest of her days. There was an odd calmness in that statement. The inevitability of fate looming, washing around her like waves on an ocean. Maybe it was destined, written in the stars, her defeat.

She couldn't defy these stars.

They were here.

TIA BLYTHE (14)
Colston's Girls' School, Bristol

The Bleeding Heart

I collapse into the bars of my cage, and am thrown backwards, unable to scream. I don't give myself time to catch my breath as I catapult into the bone structure again and again. Backwards and forwards I run, a pounding in my ears. My efforts to escape have never been rewarded yet, but still I continue. Something appears in front of me, pushing its way through darkness and I speed up, desperate to escape. The handle of the knife gets stuck in the bars of my ribcage, protecting me. I slow to a juddering, heart-stopping last beat.

Philippa Evans (14)
Colston's Girls' School, Bristol

The End

I haven't done anything. So why me? What did I do wrong? I took their advice, I said nothing, I did nothing, I made no fuss. But now they've chosen me. I'm not the first and I'm not the last.
The hand grabs me and lifts me into the air. Below lays the shredded skin of those who came before me and their blood has been splattered carelessly on the ground. Beneath me is a disturbing pile of sliced and crushed flesh, hiding a set of motionless curved blades, waiting to be activated.
It's a bitter end for Granny Smith.

Fiona Chung (14)
Colston's Girls' School, Bristol

THE GUN

The gun was cold, grey and seemingly supple in her feather-light grip. It had an aura about it; a silence, an end, barbaric and beautiful. Her painted lips formed a smile as she brought the muzzle to his head and her lacquered nails tightened on the trigger. She watched the bullet enter his skull and leave a fraction of a second later, taking blood, brain matter and bone fragments with it. Her smile widened as her husband slumped forward, blood pouring from his head.
The sharp smell of gun smoke and the coppery tang of freshly-spilt blood filled her nose.

MAISIE CALDWELL (14)
Colston's Girls' School, Bristol

SUFFOCATING

I'm suffocating.
Every breath burns my lungs as I try to get to the window. Crimson flames surround me, licking at my skin, engulfing me. My eyes sting as thick smoke continues to fill the air.
I can see the window now, a dark shadow up ahead. Hacking coughs shake through me as I double over. Dark spots dance in front of my eyes as I attempt to push myself off the ground.
It's so close now. I can almost touch it.
Mustering up my strength, I push at the glass, but it won't budge. The window is locked.

NOUR TAZAOUI (14)
Colston's Girls' School, Bristol

TRACKS

As I pounded down the rotten tracks, the dim lights flickered ominously and a ghastly stench filled my nostrils and lungs, clogging up my airways. To think she was alone in the bitter cold, defenceless and lost. Then I saw a dark silhouette lurking in the shadows. I had to reach her. Suddenly, there was a blinding light and a loud rumble racing towards us. Then a piercing scream. *Crash!* She was gone.

IMOGEN SAHNI (13)
Colston's Girls' School, Bristol

THE MIRROR

My hands aren't bleeding. But why does the mirror tell me otherwise? All I can see on my hands is skin, my skin. And yet why in the mirror are they covered in dark red blood? Why is my face covered in scars? Why can't I feel the pain that I can see? Is my reflection a lie? Am I going crazy? Have I finally succumbed to the insanity that my life has led me up to? Will I be taken away once again? But then, I see it.
I see my reflection blink.

ISABELA CORTES HYLAND (13)
Colston's Girls' School, Bristol

A BLACK STORM

It was a storm. No one was on the streets or in the houses. I was alone, in the rain. A black alley stretched for as long as I could see. Shivering, I began to see a flickering light. Like a moth to a flame, I flew towards the heat. *Splash!* Water streamed down my leg. All of a sudden, I realised someone was watching me. But who? Rapidly, I ran down the street, peering over my shoulder every five seconds; I kept running until I reached a dead end. There she was. Tall and towering, all in black.

EMILY DUNNINGHAM (12)
Colston's Girls' School, Bristol

EMPTY

I watch a hand go to her cheek, leaving trails of blood from under her fingernails, another brushstroke added to the scarlet masterpiece of her face. She doesn't wipe it away. Why should she? There'll be more. So much more. It leaks from every pore in her body, painting its crimson signature over every inch of once-perfect skin. The disease: nameless, cureless. A killer that doesn't kill. The parasite refills the empty shell's veins to become an emotionless, gruesome monstrosity. Glancing down, I notice the blooming scarlet at my fingertips. Soon, I will be walking amongst the army of undead.

PHOEBE LUCE (12)
Colston's Girls' School, Bristol

Azure Curtains, Bloody Tiles And My Hope Erased

It all came flashing back; a kaleidoscope of memories...
Running. From the ecstatic woman with the chainsaw. In hospital. I
had a broken arm. That's why I went.
Azure curtains, bloody tiles and my hope erased. Waiting anxiously
for the nurse, who arrives with her torturous chainsaw. She grins. I die
a little. We scurry around like 'Tom and Jerry' - enemies at first sight. I
dive under an isolated bed, in the hope I'm not her prey.
Then it happens again.
Running. From the ecstatic woman with the chainsaw. In hospital. I
had a broken arm. That's why I went.

Jema Ali (12)
Colston's Girls' School, Bristol

RUN!

Everyone in the theatre applauded as the ventriloquist entered the stage.
'Hello Bob, what's your favourite food?' asked the ventriloquist.
The puppet slowly turned its wooden head. 'Blood!' it shrieked, sinking its teeth into his neck.
My younger sister Abi clung to my hand. 'What's happening?' she asked.
Not answering, I picked her up and fled. We crouched in a dark alley, waiting. A rustle of leaves behind us, then Abi screamed and fell: cold. Sadness overwhelmed my soul. 'Who could do this?' I cried.
Suddenly, I felt a warm trickle of blood down my neck.
'Me!' said a voice.

ISABEL MUNDAY (11)
Colston's Girls' School, Bristol

LAST NIGHT

I ran my finger along the cracked glass, grazing the skin. The terrifying image of what had happened flashed angrily in my mind, as quickly as the blood now seeping from my finger. My fists clenched. I had had enough! What more could anyone do to pierce my heart? It was over. Devastated, I lay down. The leaves crunched beneath my weight. Silence...

A twig snapped. My eyes flickered. The air swirled mysteriously around my shoulders, whispering. I reached for my knife, but an icy hand gripped my arm. A scream span through the darkness. And a life was lost.

AVA SOAR (11)
Colston's Girls' School, Bristol

HIDE-AND-SEEK

It was a warm summer's day. I was playing hide-and-seek with my friends Jade and Libby. I was well hidden behind a leafy green bush that prickled. I shuddered and heard noises.

'Come on. Come on!' someone muttered. 'We've got to shift these items before the cops get us!'

I froze in shock. I slowly peeped out of the bush, to see two men dragging glass items from a nearby mansion furtively. Strangely, I heard no sirens, not even faintly. Oh. They were moving towards me. Suddenly, they ripped open the innocent leaves, leaving me filled with terror...

EMMA WISE (11)
Colston's Girls' School, Bristol

THE STALKER

It was cold outside. The eerie mist swirled around the dim glow of the lamp post in the moonlight. Ella wrapped her arms tightly around herself and sped up her walk. It seemed wise, she thought, to go the shorter way... through the forest.

Ten minutes later, the trees were towering above her. The only sound was the wheezing of her own breath. A twig snapped behind her. She spun round. Darkness. She carried on walking, although, she knew someone was there. She could feel their eyes watching. She took a shuddering breath.

'Hello Ella,' said a cold voice.

LIZZIE ELLIOTT (12)
Colston's Girls' School, Bristol

ECHOES OF THE FOREST

Storm clouds gather overhead, spitting out raindrops. I knew he'd run off; why do I agree to look after him? 'Henry! Henry! Henry, where are you?' I call into the gloomy, barren field.

Trees sway, completely in sync, whistling in the wind. They tower over the grass, casting shadows in the night. *Snap!* The forest. Henry. My feet kick the leaves as I run into the dead life of rotting wood. I shout for him again - but no reply.

'Emily.'

Echoes of my name race round the abandoned walls of the forest. Darkness falls over me - I whisper, 'Henry... ?'

TILLY BENNETT (12)
Colston's Girls' School, Bristol

THE WORK OF THE UNFORGOTTEN

Eek! This was how her father died! The cobbles beneath her feet rattled as she stood on them. The humid fog choked her like a thick winter blanket, holding up the heavy darkness. Kneeling over his grave, her eyes stung with tears. All her strength gathered together to prevent her from sobbing. It wouldn't work. A stray tear meandered down her face, and it hit the floor. A cold hand grabbed her shoulder; she gasped in horror, it was her dad! Amy's last words; a scream, as she was dragged into the darkness, the darkness of the past...

MEENA MORRIS (11)
Colston's Girls' School, Bristol

MY DEADLY DREAM

I thought it was all a dream. Blood dripping off the walls, creepy footsteps. Nobody was in the house apart from me. Who could it be? I opened the door. What was it? A silhouette of some sort. It was holding something strange. Was it an axe, a hatchet or a sword? No one could tell.
All of a sudden, it started moving towards me. I stepped back, scared of what was going to happen. My heart pounded, sweat dripped down my forehead. I tried to open the door behind me. It wouldn't open. What was I going to do?

LAUREN JAY CONNOLLY (12)
Colston's Girls' School, Bristol

CATECHISM

Whenever Gillian got asked why he asked so many questions, he would just smile and reply with, 'Curiosity, experiment, resolution, test and retest.'
There was silence all afternoon before Gillian arrived.
'Mum, how long would it take for earthworms to decompose a body?'
Mum sighed; the bliss was shattered once again with inconsequential inquiries. 'I don't know love.' Mum heard Gillian opening the drawer. The image of the crater in the backyard came into her mind. She turned to see that the sharpest knife had disappeared from the drawer.
'I'm sorry Mum, I really need to know the answer... '
Silence.

MEGHA RAECHAL BIJOY (15)
Colston's Girls' School, Bristol

MY OBITUARY

I open my eyes but all I see is darkness. I blink but it makes no difference. Where am I? I'm lying on my back. I try to move but realise I'm confined; trapped. My fingertips can feel the cold dampness of gnarly wood and a stench of wet earth fills my nostrils. Panic swells inside me but I know I must stay calm and think of a way to get out of this nightmare. As my brain races, the deathly silence is suddenly shattered by a sickening thud as earth crashes down above me... I'm in a coffin!

THEA ROSE CLARKE (11)
Colston's Girls' School, Bristol

THE SEARCH

She closed the door. A solitary bulb hung limply in the corner, bathing the room in a dim, wavering light. Long streaks of crimson stained the gritty walls. She shivered. In the centre of the room a charred iron throne stood proud, rusted chains snaking along the arms. Beads of sweat glimmering on her forehead, she inched closer. Suddenly, the crack of electricity. This was a sophisticated torture device. The icy silence froze her. She had nowhere to go, but no desperate refugee would ever shelter here. She turned to run. *Bang!* Darkness. There was no one she could trust...

LILY GILCHRIST (11)
Colston's Girls' School, Bristol

WHO'S THE GHOST?

The skeletal trees tapped on the girl's window tauntingly. She ducked her head under the duvet in fear. Then, the tapping grew louder and more persistent. She looked up slowly to realise it was someone knocking on her door. Gingerly, she walked over and opened it to see a dark figure running down the stairs. Scared, she shut it again, locking it this time and turned around to see her own lifeless body sprawled across the bed, a knife sticking out and her eyes bulging. She looked down at her pale, transparent ghostly hands and her bloodstained nightdress.

AMARA WILLIS (12)
Colston's Girls' School, Bristol

THE NIGHT STALKER

It was coming. Faintly, I could hear the front door rattling; bushes shaking, heavy breathing and deep footsteps that made the ground wobble violently. Quickly, I sprinted up the stairs like a lightning bolt. Fearfully, I locked my bedroom door, hoping that the creature wouldn't be able to open it; I blocked it with my chair just in case. Suddenly, the front door opened with a bang. The floor creaked as the door slammed shut. My heart was pounding; I knew that I was going to be dead in a few seconds. There was no time left, because now...

YARA HANA MCKINEN (12)
Colston's Girls' School, Bristol

MY CHILDMINDER

I told them no. 'Don't go!' I said. They ignored me. A few days later, I found myself alone with her. 'Her' is my childminder. If you can call her that. I know she is evil. She doesn't like children: she hates them. Her ferocious eyes and dark wild hair can only mean... my childminder is a witch!
I heard her footsteps, ever so slowly, creeping up the stairs. I listened to the silence as loud as one hundred voices. I stared through the darkness, shaking. The door slowly opened. She gave a deranged cackle then aimed her wand...

MAISIE DODD (12)
Colston's Girls' School, Bristol

THE PLAYGROUND

The screeching of the swing pierces my ears. My brain tells me to run. My heart tells me to stay. A ghostly figure appears from around, shaded by the mist. My heart begins to panic. Seesaw, seesaw. Over and over in my head I can hear voices all around me; telling me to do this, telling me to do that. What to do. Crouch. Everything stops. My eyes open. Head slowly lifts. *Bang!*
Darkness. Children are running around, singing happy songs. My heart warms as the children play. I remember when I was like that, so fragile, so sweet.

KAMARA FORREST (14)
Colston's Girls' School, Bristol

SMOKE

I am alone right now. The rich oaky smell of the fire permeated the room, wisps of silver-grey smoke curled and danced their way through the thick hazy air, as if excited to escape the gentle pull of the chimney. Even after the fire had long been extinguished, the smoky smell would linger on the fabric of the chairs, on the curtains and on the carpets. It hung on the air, ready to greet whoever opened the front door seeking to escape the bitter gusts of winter wind that howled around the cottage at this time of year.

ZEINAB ISMAACIL (14)
Colston's Girls' School, Bristol

THE END

I made another futile attempt to pick myself up off the ground. No use. My classmates were all laid down, presumably unconscious. My head was throbbing, trying to make an understanding of what had happened, as well as dealing with a massive bleed. I pushed the table off me, and with the last of my strength, I thrust all my weight onto a chair facing the smashed window which separated me from the main road. It was at that moment I saw it. Buildings were engulfed in flames and a blanket of dust covered the roads. This was the end.

TRINITY WILLIS (13)
Colston's Girls' School, Bristol

THE TRAIN RIDE

I walked through the deserted train carriage, my hair sweeping the silver cobwebs. I heard a piercing scream echo throughout, cold blood dripped mysteriously from above. Bluntly, I looked up and saw a head hanging from a rope, blood pouring out of the eyes and ears. Bruises covered the forehead and its eyes were pure white. I stood there in shock, not knowing what to do. I remember being chased to the rusty doors and leaping out of the moving train. After that, all I remember was falling off a rocky cliff, plunging into the water and passing out.

AMIRA SHAKOOR (13)
Colston's Girls' School, Bristol

The Revenge Of The Mortals

Her vibrant blue eyes blinked in the deathly horror, for the first time in decades.

As her bleak sandals twitched, smoke erupted and rose dismally to meet the milky sky. A single tear fell from its solid state to finally meet her cracked lips.

An 'O' shape met her mouth, and her doll-like hair fell around her pale ears. Everything had changed.

The tombstones were gone, replaced with magnificent wonders of which only pure mortals would have the stupidity to create, and she knew it.

So this was their revenge. It was time for hers, and she was ready...

ISABELLE HATTON-WILLIAMS (11)
Colston's Girls' School, Bristol

Circus Freak

I couldn't take my eyes off the face in the shop window: frizzy, crimson hair; a bulbous scarlet nose, cold black eyes rimmed with meaty pink and a large blood-red smile plastered over his flour-white face. Continuing my journey home, the shadows enclosed me in a pitch-black corridor. Somewhere behind me, I heard footsteps: getting louder and faster. Silence. Suddenly the footsteps were in front of me. Panic-stricken, I rushed to my gate. I looked up at the window. I stared in disbelief and a shiver ran through me. Staring at me were cold black eyes rimmed with meaty pink...

UNA JEAN JENKINS (12)
Colston's Girls' School, Bristol

THE MYSTERIOUS ALLEYWAY

All alone on the alleyway, stood the stone of death. If anyone disobeyed they would be slaughtered.

One day, a young schoolgirl was lost and before she knew it, she found herself hanging from a tree seconds away from death. Blood poured and dripped out of her flesh. She screamed a scream of pain so loud you jumped when she blasted her distress out of her lungs. It was clear about what had happened, she did the unprecedented, the never done before, and before we knew it, in front of our own eyes, the young girl died.

ZAINA KAFIENAH (11)
Colston's Girls' School, Bristol

THE MYSTERY MAN

I stood by the stairs, freezing in pyjamas.

'Ava, hurry.'

I would love something mysterious to happen, I thought. I ruffled open the purple, silky curtains. My eyes swivelled over to a black face eyeing me out the window. 'OMG.' I raced upstairs into bed. Waking sweaty, I glanced at Cousin Ava. 'Argh!' Her head tilted, mist billowed out of her 'O' shaped mouth, followed by her insides.

A black figure stood over her. I couldn't contain myself. My blood fizzed. I rocked myself, trying to understand the situation. W... was I mad? What was happening to me?

HANNAN MOHAMED NASSOR (11)
Colston's Girls' School, Bristol

You'll Never Be Alone

It was a foggy night and the sky was dark and gloomy. I had told Mother earlier, 'I'll be in by eight.' It was getting close to nine and I knew Mother would be worried. There was expected storms and lightning. Trees were swaying. Telegraph poles falling. It all felt like a nightmare.

As I cautiously walked up our street leading to my house, I paused and looked around me, faint voices coming from all directions. I felt as if I was being watched. The weather was getting worse so I carried on slowly walking. I was scared, shadows! Darkness!

Amy Higgs (13)
Huish Episcopi Academy, Langport

The Mirror

Once there was a mirror in an old abandoned warehouse which was delivered to a massive manor. This was no *ordinary* mirror, it showed how you were going to die!

There was a man called Jason. Jason lived in the manor and he also owned the mirror. His friend came to visit, looked in the mirror and saw his neck getting slit! He then saw himself drowning in his own blood! You could see the killer's face, so Jason went to find the killer to do what he did to his friend; *slit his throat and watch him die slowly!!*

Ciaran Dowling (14)
Huish Episcopi Academy, Langport

STROKE AFTER MIDNIGHT

It was my daughter's birthday. I gave her a doll to go in her doll's house. We noticed the light flicker then the doll was gone. 'Did you drop it?' I questioned, but then I felt like something was watching me. Later that night, I heard noises from downstairs and then again on the stairs I thought I heard faint voices.
We woke up the next morning, our little girl was dead. We tried to wake her, she wouldn't wake. We looked around for anything that could've killed her, we found a knife... then had that feeling of being watched...

EDWARD WHITE (13)
Huish Episcopi Academy, Langport

THE APOCALYPSE

It was day three, the cold, wet rain poured down my face. I crept into the abandoned factory, hoping it was empty. I knew that I was the last in my city. All my family were gone, either they'd fled or were killed. I ran down the hall and opened a rusty door into the locker room. 'Hello?' I called...
Suddenly, 'Argh!' A loud scream.
I started to run but a hand grabbed me and pulled me in. I was surrounded by zombies, I reached for my gun quickly, but all I felt was a sharp pain in my neck.

BETH DAVIES
Huish Episcopi Academy, Langport

A Silent Scream

I've seen him. The face, the hair. He was here. His shadow following me around the room, I heard my heart pounding, the squeaking of the floorboards. He was out to get me. Suddenly, I felt a wind rush over me; a big bony hand had gently touched my shoulder. My spine shivered and I felt my body shaking. He slowly turned me around until I was facing him head on. There was no way out. I struggled for freedom, he had a firm grip, it was useless. I finally gave up struggling. He had caught me.

MEGAN HARRIS (13)
Huish Episcopi Academy, Langport

The Boneyard

It was a damp, gloomy night and little Timmy was stuck in a graveyard. Little Timmy felt a tapping on his shoulder, it made him jump out of his skin. He turned, he saw it was a tree branch tapping on him. He walked through the graveyard. He heard a *croak!* and a green slimy creature jumped out. It was a frog! Little Timmy was relieved that it was just a silly frog. He thought it was a witch but Timmy knew witches didn't exist. He sneaked through the graveyard, heard a cackle, he turned around... It was a witch!

KIERAN ARMSTRONG (14)
Huish Episcopi Academy, Langport

THE BABY KILLER

As I checked on my dear baby Charlotte, I realised that it was dark. Too dark. I switched on the light, it wouldn't work. Then, as I turned around I saw splatters all over the wall like a bloodshot-red. Suddenly it occurred to me, could she be... ? No of course she couldn't. As I approached the cradle, my nerves were building and building, however as I looked over I saw... a lump under the covers. I composed myself then stretched my arm across to the cover. I pulled it back. Oh my dear Charlotte, she was... gone!

ROSE WHEELER (13)
Huish Episcopi Academy, Langport

AWAY FROM HOME

I was in a dark, gloomy forest, it was 4:30am, I was cold, scared and sad. I'd just run away from home. I had no food or water, not even a mobile phone! I decided to run far, far away to get through the forest and thought I'd find a road or something, but as I walked I realised that the forest never ended. I got really scared and sad so I started to freak out and quickly started to sprint back the way I came, but then I stopped, my big, beloved house wasn't even there!

WILLIAM CARTWRIGHT (13)
Huish Episcopi Academy, Langport

The Shadow

One night I was sat my room and heard stones at my window. I went to look and there was no one there. I went downstairs to have a look. I could see a man in all black, like a shadow. I went outside with a flashlight to look around. There was a rustle in the bushes. I got a stick and poked around. I heard a cat hiss and growl, something like a wave of relief.
All of a sudden, I heard a glass smash. I ran inside, only to see the horror before me, it was him... !

Grace Perrott (13)
Huish Episcopi Academy, Langport

Maths Class

It was the beginning of December. I was dared to enter my school at night, stupid me took up the dare. I walked to the main door, hanging off its hinges. 'Huh, what happened?' I continued down the corridors as the light flickered. I carried on walking until my foot hit a small handle. I went to pull it but then I heard a screech. I turned around to look. It was the door moving on impact of the wind. I turned around and I saw a dark face appear. I heard the school bell.
'Wake up!'
Maths was over.

Patryk Wojton (13)
Huish Episcopi Academy, Langport

You'll Never Be Alone

One evening the young, blonde girl (Sami) woke up in the middle of nowhere, vulnerable and abandoned. She only remembered drinking in her bedroom because she couldn't understand the meaning of life. She stood up to see a strange figure, it was a see-through woman in a bright white dress. She began to walk. Sami screamed, 'Help!' Sami then ran after her but the more she ran the less of the woman she could see. She approached an old arch with a smashed window. she dropped dead and the ghostly woman began to drag her into eternal darkness.

SCOTT GRANT
Huish Episcopi Academy, Langport

The Killensies On Planet Zebrin

Night-time on Zebrin is anarchy, especially for the Killensies. A race so eager to kill you, you would blink and you're dead. They're shadows, apart from two pupil-less eyes. Once, they built an army so great no other race on Zebrin could face it. They began to march, slowly but surely, to the Underworld, home of the Quinnlings, a race of good. They were not unprepared. They had assembled a small army, ready for battle. The Killensies charged, and all that could be heard was the screams of the fallen. War declared, only time will tell the Quinnlings' fate.

MATTY WYLIE (11)
Kingswood School, Bath

Up The Stairs And Beyond

Ahead, in the blur of darkness, spills out rays of light concealed behind a firm door; restricting any hope of life beyond. Behind, only the solemn gloom of the unknown dragging me onward, away from that recurring nightmare. Halfway up. Surely by now it's too late? With each trembling step upon each creaking stair the knocking grows stronger, the whispers louder. I know that knocking pattern. I recognise that frail whisper, yet they're so unfamiliarly resentful, brisk and murderous. The time is as near as I am to that shining door, until the ghostly hand grasps me. I fall.

DAVIDA SAMIKWA (13)
Kingswood School, Bath

I Can't Get No Satisfaction

The skin was cold. She eased her nails into the neck's skin; watching it blush red like the modesty of an ugly child. She grunted, her energy pulsing through to his skin; still to no avail. Could she not be satisfied? What a damn thick neck. He obviously played sport. Embarrassed, she allowed her fingers to languish over the squirming veins, like she was playing the harp. His screams were pitchy, goddammit. She once again gripped, still feeling cold satisfaction from the touch. Before she could wink, the cold lost its breeze. She must have pressed too hard. Oops.

RÓISÍN TAPPONI (16)
Kingswood School, Bath

I Knew My Job

Death. That smell. The smell of death. It lingered in the air. I stared down at the body. A face that was once filled with life and emotion, a face that had colour and spirit, a face, empty, a shell. The colour had seeped out with the blood and the life had vanished. The empty pod that was once seen as a human lay there. I knew what I had done. I knew what I must do. I knew. This person was now history. A former life. It was my job, as its killer. It was my job to vanish.

HARRY WARNE (16)
Kingswood School, Bath

Escape

Creaking, crunching, slithering and sliding it stood, waiting, watching. As silent as a mouse it went closer and closer, until finally it reached the stairs, clambering up it went to the top of the house, scratching against the wooden floor. Nail-biting, we waited for the shadows to descend down upon us. The looming darkness was near, as the wind whistled in fear. Try not to make a sound, otherwise to Heaven my friend. *Tip, tap* the door went. Faces stopped as hard as stones in trepidation and apprehension. What was this creature? Only the stuff of nightmares or fantasy?

CHARLOTTE CROWE (16)
Kingswood School, Bath

THE BEASTS OF A DEADLY DIALECT

In the dark there's one thing that unites us all; lurking in the shadows are creatures of death, cursed to haunt the living for eternity. Ancient beasts that inhabit our world, and have done for aeons, they live in plain sight and await the chance to hook their claws around our fragile hearts. They originate from the darkness of a dead language, and are enslaved by these words. When they are close; the human heart beats frantically, our palms sweat, and the pressure rides on the chest. But they can only catch you if you look. You are their prey…

EVE BURCH (17)
Kingswood School, Bath

HANGING ON

Looking at my reflection, I wasn't surprised by the lack of warmth or emotion. My lips, slightly parted, were tinted purple and my nose was indistinguishable from the rest of my milky skin. My hair's neatly taken back, to create a perfect sphere on the top of my head, with only a few stray stands gently floating by my forehead. My eyes once duck-egg blue were bloodshot-red. My reflection swayed from side to side and my body gracefully elevated by the braided knot that hung from the light bulb centred on the high-rise chalky-white ceiling above.

JESSE AKIWUMI (16)
Kingswood School, Bath

Bonfire Fright

I like Bonfire Night. Every year I celebrate by parading around, but this year was different. As I rounded the final bend towards the bonfire, a decrepit lady asked me, 'Would you like some toffee?' Her face was so welcoming that I agreed. Suddenly, my arms felt wooden and I could no longer move. A sly smile creased along her thin lips. 'Come here children!' she cooed. 'The guy is ready.'
'Thank you, Mrs Mephisto,' cried a swarm of children as they carried me towards the pile of planks. As I was placed atop the mound, the orange glow appeared...

Henry McCollom (13)
Kingswood School, Bath

New Dawn Gone

A sudden drop in temperature made him aware of an unwelcome presence in his bedroom. Immobilised, he felt it come closer; without hope, he stared ahead. The breath on his cheek stole around his face like snakes and each inhalation drained his will. A hand crept around him from behind. The persistent fingers slipped across his neck like a cold noose. Determination for a new dawn gone, the fingers straightened his tie. He hung his head and looked at his wife. The day set to progress, as every other.

Maddy Attwood (13)
Kingswood School, Bath

UNTITLED

It was night in our new house. The tree outside my room cast shadows onto my walls. Suddenly, there was a loud bang on my door. I quivered under my bed in fear. The door flew open. The face came towards me. It was the same face that was in the book of cannibal killers I was reading earlier. Suddenly, I felt a sharp pain on my neck. I glanced down to see that my body had gone…

NICK BAINES (14)
Kingswood School, Bath

THE COTTAGE

It was dark. They snaked their way through the trees to reach the cottage. They were hand in hand, moving as fast as they could. They reached the cottage, it stood before them. Something wasn't right, the door was open, the light was on, the oven door was open with a doll holding a note, it said one thing: 'Run'. The girl pulled at the boy's sleeve to leave but he was too intrigued. The men approached the cottage appearing from the tree wielding a variety of weapons. They snaked their way through the trees to reach the cottage…

JOE DANIEL WHITE (13)
Kingswood School, Bath

PLAYTIME

The children crept into the gloomy room and then the light flickered on and a doll appeared on a chair, with one of its eyes missing. As they started heading towards the door it swiftly shut in one motion. When they looked back at the chair the doll was gone and now there was a note on it. It read: 'Come and play with me'. The kids froze in fear, then heard the door, which was shut, open behind them. Then they heard from a high-pitched voice, 'Do you want to play with me?' 'Friends…'

JOE GOULD (12)
Kingswood School, Bath

I KNOW YOU'RE AWAKE...

Ding-dong. 2am. Footsteps outside my door. I pretend to be asleep, hoping it's my parents. The door creaks open and a shadow snakes across my wall. Is it a murderer? It has something shiny… Is that a knife? *Screech!* I shut my eyes. Silence… I raise an eyelid. Petrifying words are engraved on the wall: 'I know you're awake!' Terrified, I shrink under the covers, praying I am safe. Worries freeze in my head, shivers run through my body. Silence… I force my head out and I stare straight into two blood-curdling, hellish eyes… 'Argh!'

HELENA BRAIN (12)
Kingswood School, Bath

THE SEWER

Mertha fell. When she hit the bottom she felt the liquid, it was gooey and felt like mucus. Mertha got out of the weird substance and kept walking down the sewers. *I can't believe those girls threw me down here!* she thought to herself. She kept walking, she heard splashing around the corner. She peered round the corner and she saw a creature who seemed unbelievably strong. She ran. Mertha kept running, saw another one chasing her coming from another section of the sewers. She then saw a door, she wasn't sure whether to go in or not…

NATHAN BODE (12)
Kingswood School, Bath

A FEW MOMENTS LATER…

'They told me to stay on the line for as long as I could.'
A few moments later she got a phone call from the police. It made her jump. She spoke to the chief constable who said, 'It's okay, we have a team coming to your house now.' But they were too late. By the time they got to her house she was gone. They listened to a voicemail. It was him. The one who took her. It said, 'I have taken her, if you want her back, you will have to come and find me… '

KEIRA MILLIE HARDEN (12)
Kingswood School, Bath

BENEATH THE DIRT

Mary Hall was highly intelligent. However, on Friday the 13th she went into the gloomy, gruesome graveyard of Kinderton. The metal gates screamed as they swung open, echoing like volcanoes into the distance. Mary stopped in her tracks in front of a grave reading: 'Mary Hall, 1972-1983, car accident'. A hand appeared to be reaching out, as if crying for help. Was it Mary's hand? If so, who was looming above it? The heartbeat of its watch went tick-tock, echoing through its brain as voices tormented it, screeches piercing its ears till there was only silence and pure darkness.

BETH HARRIS (13)
Kingswood School, Bath

MIDNIGHT MOVEMENTS

All of a sudden, she awoke. It was midnight and all the clocks were striking twelve. As well as the chiming bells, a low, rumbling noise was coming from downstairs. The young girl took a tentative step out of bed; the floorboards creaked. Trying hard to ignore the sounds, she crept downstairs. The moon cast shadows, the old grandfather clock ticked. Something was going on. As she drew closer to the kitchen door she heard a groaning noise. Putting her hand on the door, she started to make out threatening, individual words. She opened the door…

LOUISE BEDDING (12)
Kingswood School, Bath

Keyhole

He never wanted to. Of course he didn't. It was because of the baby and its 'requirements'. He had never needed to move when he was a baby. Then I guess he wasn't anything like that baby. Then it happened, his family moved into a dilapidated house in York. Johnny had loved his old bedroom. This new one was strange and what was that door? It wasn't on the plans, in fact it didn't even have a handle, just a keyhole. His new sibling slept upstairs so why could he hear giggling? And what was its cause?

SAM BERNSTEIN (13)
Kingswood School, Bath

Screeching

After hours of travelling, he'd arrived. Driving up the lane was scary. It was gloomy; bare black branches, thunder and lightning roaring, and the wind whistling. The door creaked open to the house. The cobwebs wiped over his face as he fumbled for his torch. His torch didn't work. The door slammed behind and plunged him into the darkness. He turned to open the door. Something grabbed onto his back, its claws digging into his shoulders. Something screeching into his ears while his heart was racing. Fear overtook him and he dived for the door…

GEORGE SMITH (12)
Kingswood School, Bath

IT IS TIME...

We moved into our new home. Something didn't feel right. I was left
with the room at the top of the house.
After a long day of unpacking, I went to my room. As I closed the
door I heard a voice. A child's voice. 'Time for bed.' A sinister laugh
followed. Then I heard footsteps. Her face was as grey as death and
she was wielding a carving knife. She whispered, 'Time to die.'

TOM LANE FOX (12)
Kingswood School, Bath

I AM ALWAYS THERE

Anne woke up realising that she was the only person left in the world,
nothing was working. Television was scrambled, not a single noise
outside apart from her breath in the cold winter. Walking around
her house, looking at her pictures with her family and friends, but
they were all gone, forever. She looked out of the window to see
a beautiful morning with the sun rising, but all ruined in the sense
that she was alone, and it was like she was in a town full of ghosts.
Suddenly, she heard a knock at the door…

CAMERON CROWHURST (12)
Kingswood School, Bath

Burial Thoughts

We made a vow, did we not? You broke it though. You broke it by being with another person. I hated you for it, but only whilst I considered the many vows we made together. I had to think about what was fair. It is fair for me to to keep my promises so I shall. As I dig up the dirt now, making space for you both to rest in peace, I know I have kept every single vow up until the very last: "Til death do us part'.

Katie Eayres
Kingswood School, Bath

The Last Thing

The last thing I saw was my alarm clock, with its fluorescent red numbers flashing 12:07am, before she pushed her long, sharp, rotting nails through my bare throat, hooking her claws around my jugular, her other hand, cold and lifeless, muffling my desperate screams. I sat bolt upright, panting, with cold sweat dripping down my forehead, relieved it was only a dream, but as I saw my alarm clock read 12:06am, I heard my closet door creak open. 'Only a dream?' she asked, showing her ghastly fingernails as she reached around the door, opening it slowly, she whispered softly...

Christy Teal Judd (17)
Kingswood School, Bath

IS IT?

She asks the boy, 'Let's play a game!' The boy nods. 'You can be the wolf and I'll be a sheep.' He gestures again. 'Close your eyes, count to ten and find me!' The boy does this, and the girl runs.
After ten seconds he runs into the forest after her… One of the adults at the party smirks as she watches them run off. 'Oh, your boy is just too generous, playing with his little sister like that,' she says.
The mother of the girl quickly sticks her head out of the kitchen window. 'What? She has no brother!'

MAX LINES (16)
Kingswood School, Bath

TOO PRETTY

Diving into alleyways. My night. Running after shadows. Watching. Waiting. Then she appears. Too pretty for me. Too pretty for the world. She walks on. Swaying. Humming. So beautiful, too pretty for me. I take her hand. She smiles. Too pretty. I lie her down in bed. She squirms when I push the hair out of her eyes, more when I kiss her. Face, neck, shoulders. Too pretty. She gasps, whimpers a little. It takes only a minute. She felt no pain. I threw the knife in the river. She is too pretty for me. Too pretty for the world.

ELIZABETH SCOTT (16)
Kingswood School, Bath

EYES

The church stood tall and foreboding. It stared down, trying to intimidate me. I entered through the large wooden door which made a loud creak as if a thousand years had passed since it last opened. I tiptoed down the dusty aisle, making no noise. At the altar stood a tall, dark silhouette. 'You're here!' the figure spoke and I jumped with fright. His voice was low and gravelly. He turned around and the first thing I noticed were his eyes. Dark, powerful and almost as if fires were burning in sunken sockets. No! Wait! They were fire! I ran.

ELLIE VAID (13)
Kingswood School, Bath

THE BABYSITTER AND THE LULLABY

Last night, I was babysitting for a very rich family. They had a grand house, however silence reigned over. I sat on their sofa, bored, the baby monitor by my side, the house empty. Eventually, I decided to break the eerie silence by turning the TV on. As soon as I turned it on the baby started crying, I decided to wait and see if she would calm down. Then I heard a lullaby coming through the baby monitor. I was stunned, afraid. Immediately, I called the parents and the police. They arrived, stormed the baby's room, but found nothing…

JAMIE DEVERELL (13)
Kingswood School, Bath

THE CLOAKED MAN

My body froze to the spot. He was staring like a madman, right into my eyes. He wore a draped black cape covering his muscular frame. Black gloves covered his brutish hands. In his right hand was a knife. Its blade glinting in the moonlight, curled into a deadly tip as sharp as a needle, but as strong as steel. His eyes were lifeless, except the glint of the Devil's face looking through his soul. His facial features were far from perfect. Suddenly, he charged like an enraged bull, with only one thing on his mind - to kill me.

STEPHEN KING (13)
Kingswood School, Bath

SLY PLUM LIPS

Light blinded me, yet I couldn't see through the shrouding shadows of the space. Suddenly, an image flashed on and the silhouette of sly, plum lips appeared. 'I have seen you. I have seen you with them, take us to them. Take us to them all.' The voice was solid and had a hint of a French accent. What she'd said made sense, but I do not stand for disloyalty. I heard a trickle of water, soon my ankles were submerged. Slowly, it crept up past my knees, then to my lower chest. Then I understood. 'Yes, I'll do it.'

HARRIET FOSTER (14)
Kingswood School, Bath

FACES

He ran down the shadowy corridor. He couldn't shake the feeling that he had been this way before. He flitted past the portraits of his predecessors, then turned the corner. Wait… Hadn't he just passed his grandfather's portrait? He ran frantically round another corner and again the same portraits, but now they were in different positions. He became exhausted as he turned corner after corner, each time the same faces, taunting, mocking. Panic plagued his face. His vision clouded. He slumped opposite his grandfather. The walls closed in. As he blacked out, the face of the old man laughing, laughing...

NOAH SMALL (13)
Kingswood School, Bath

ALONE

Fog steamed up the rain-drenched windowpane, obscuring the view; I peered out, pressing my face to the glass. Rain hammered down and the glacial glass sent chills down my spine. About to turn away, I noticed a movement through the torrent outside. A face appeared, white painted, black-pitted eyes and a wide grinning smile. Rain smeared his mask like his eyes were bleeding. He bore his eyes into my soul. Raising his hand to the window, he pressed his finger to the glass, that moment I realised he wasn't looking at me, but at my child, stood, distant, isolated, alone.

ASHLEY HUNT (16)
Kingswood School, Bath

THE BOYS, THE THING AND THE HOUSE!

I can't find him. He has vanished, from right under my nose. My knees are cut from kneeling on the rough floor crying for him. I stumble into the room directly opposite me in the hallway, with flickering lights and a constant smell of decay. As I slowly open the door, I begin to see Josh, tied to the bed at the other end of the room in the dark. The door quietly creaks to a close behind me and then I feel a gentle breeze down my thin neck. It is now that I realise we aren't alone!

HARVEY BROOKS (13)
Kingswood School, Bath

GRANDMA'S HOUSE

A young child was sleeping in her grandma's old house. It was said to be haunted but she'd never believed anything her dad said. The night she was staying at her grandma's, her parents had gone to see a theatre production. No lights on, like they weren't at home. Her grandma was sleeping on the other side of the house so there was no way she was walking over there. Unfortunately, she needed a pee. It was halfway down the spooky corridor. She got out of bed then *flash!* and she was back in her cosy bed.

MAX MOHR (13)
Kingswood School, Bath

THE UNKNOWN

Darkness crept over the night sky, I needed to get home before twelve!
I walked through the abandoned hallway of the old train station!
A cool atmosphere hit my face like an autumn breeze! 'Hello, is anyone there?' There was no reply. Suddenly, a laugh came galloping towards me like a lion running for its prey!
'Don't be afraid of me!' a deep voice giggled!
I ran and ran until I stopped. Somehow, my heart felt as if it had been ripped out of my body!
'Help… help me!' I screamed, a heavy breath warmed up my neck. 'Argh!'

SOPHIE JANE LEVY (13)
Stanchester Academy, Stoke-Sub-Hamdon

THE ROCK - ALCATRAZ

It was the morning of Friday 4th December in Alcatraz. The Rock. Prisoners and staff awoke to the shivering sound of death and torture, lingering like an awful stench travelling through. Apprehensive and scared, the governor anxiously ran towards 'Cell Block B' (solitary confinement). Death. Disembowelled bodies littered the cell block, dripping with haemoglobin-clogged blood. 'Run!' exclaimed the half-eaten body of 'The Birdman'! Suddenly, all the other remains shouted, 'Run!' as if it was a choir of death. Silently lurking around the corner was the murderer. Confronted by fear and anxiety, the unambiguous warden slowly fell. Dead.

SEBASTIAN WOODWARD
The Kings Of Wessex Academy, Cheddar

THE CLOAK ON THE ABBEY

The fire blazed ferociously. I felt the warmth on my face. Gone. My love, gone. I wanted to run but I was frozen. As I stared at my trembling fingers, something dark shot past me in the orange gloom. Swiftly, I glanced up, wiped my eyes. I stepped lightly over the shattered stained glass windows, ensuring not to cut myself. I couldn't bear to pass his burning body. Firefighters rushed past me, almost pushing my limp body to the floor. That's when I saw it. I found the dark figure. She smirked. Suddenly, she disappeared. No trace left behind.

LAURA GILVEAR
The Kings Of Wessex Academy, Cheddar

I'LL NEVER FORGET

I will never forget that night. I'll never forget her face. Blood was trickling down her face, dripping off her chin. My friend's lifeless body behind her. The woods were the Devil's soul and the trees were looming over me. She was growling at me. I reached carefully for my torch and I turned it on. It shone in her eyes and she let out an ear-wrenching screech that showed off her bloodstained, razor-blade teeth. I ran, fear pulsing through my body…

JASMINE WOOD (15)
The Kings Of Wessex Academy, Cheddar

WHAT LIES ABOVE?

Drip. Drip. Drip. The door ahead seemed to be chanting my name as I felt myself stutter slowly towards it. Step by step. Every wooden panel underneath my feet seemed to cry a woman's mourn as my body gradually froze with fright and sadness. Wrapping my fingers around the icy handle, I turned the stiff knob and pushed the door wide open. Nothing. Nothing but an old, desolate room. Dust even filled the atmosphere, making me feel dazed and dizzy. *Drip. Drip. Drip.* I looked up to uncover the horror. I knew I wasn't alone…

IMOGEN LOW
The Kings Of Wessex Academy, Cheddar

REVENGE

It had been five years since Carl committed that crime. He murdered his best friend Nick in cold blood. He had flashbacks and visions of Nick coming back and haunting him. It played with Carl's mind as if Nick was working the strings of a puppet. As the days went by it drove Carl increasingly insane. Carl felt like he was constantly being followed. Constantly being watched. He told himself that Nick was dead and wasn't coming back. As the days went on, nights got longer but everything got worse when he saw Nick at the end of his bed…

SAM NEAL
The Kings Of Wessex Academy, Cheddar

STEEL DOORS

I approached the desolate church, witnessing a corridor of darkness before my terror-stricken eyes; children's names scraped meticulously onto steel doors. It teemed with wheelchairs, casts and diaries, discarded by infants 'healed' by God. It was charming, yet disturbing.

Fear ran through my veins, like the burning of an icy blizzard. My blood ran cold.

To my horror, 'possessed' was scribed in blood; warm, dripping blood. I was captured behind a steel door. Children crammed into every inch of capacity. They weren't normal. They were possessed; screeching in torment.

Now only my name remains, scraped meticulously onto a steel door…

ELLIE JONES (15)
The Kings Of Wessex Academy, Cheddar

SPUKHAFT HOUSE

The first thing one notices about Spukhaft House is the gaping hole in the roof. You might think that this hole was created by poor craftsmanship, or other perfectly normal causes. It's not, I'm afraid. The hole in the roof at Spukhaft House was created by… well, we're not too sure. What we do know is that there were screams. There was blood, too. The police were called, and they fled about.
The house went missing ever so suddenly. Quite strange. The other thing about Spukhaft House was that no one went back. Not while *it* lives there.

ARCHIE KENNEDY (15)
The Kings Of Wessex Academy, Cheddar

DEATH WOODS

Within the dark, gloomy woods I was running yet crouched low; seizing my chance from coming face-to-face with the beast. I came around the corner yet the giant black beast stood there like a proud headmaster. Its head was a lump of meat and its skin was a layer of waxy resin. I screamed at the top of my pitch. Its monstrous claws fiercely grabbed me; it opened its mouth, teeth shiny like in a toothpaste advert and took my head. My life had gone from strolling in the isolated, misty woods, to inside a creature's slimy intestines.

HAMISH CLARKE
The Kings Of Wessex Academy, Cheddar

Untitled

A darkness descended upon the forest, tall trees blocked out the moon's light. My footsteps seemed deafening in that unbreakable silence. Suddenly, a mind-breaking, inhuman scream ripped through the air like a bullet through soft sinews. Spinning around, looking further down the path I'd walked… I saw it. The darkness. Such a being, whose mere presence would rend your very mind in two. I ran. The fear consumed me, heart pounding, I sprinted, fuelled by adrenaline. But it wasn't enough. It had me, like the thousands before me. Another screaming voice, lost in the dark.

JOE HANCOCK (14)
The Kings Of Wessex Academy, Cheddar

Control

Thunder and lightning was all he could hear, scared to death, the little boy prayed for his life as the dark, mysterious shadow erred closer and closer. Screaming for his life the boy hoped and hoped, *is this a dream?* he asked himself, *or is it reality?* Metres away, nothing he could do. Begging and begging, the boy heard a deafening cry. *Creak, creak, creak.* The floorboards made it that much more intensifying. The ice-dark shadow was literally touching him… until it was in him. Dusky smoke filled the room; the boy was no longer in control.

ANDRÉ LEON FROST (14)
The Kings Of Wessex Academy, Cheddar

THE SCREAMING HALLWAYS

As I walked down the dimly lit, narrow corridor; I heard screeches from the walls, almost as if they were screams but not quite, like they were muffled. I continued to walk down the passageway with no light at the end, only to find myself at a dead end; I could either go left or right, as the light swung from side to side above me. I looked down the two opposing corridors, one with more screams, one without. The right corridor screeching and made of oak, whilst the left silent and concrete, which way should I turn?

LAWRENCE STEVEN
The Kings Of Wessex Academy, Cheddar

DEATH MINE

Picking up his old, battered lamp the boy legged it towards the exit of the mine; the thing that was chasing him was grotesque and dangerous, that was all he knew. He also knew that if it caught up with him he would be dead. Previous victims littered the floor; some were old, some fresh, creating a smell of rotting corpses that perforated his nose. This combined together, made a feeling of terrible dread-induced nausea. The exit was in sight… *Slash.* Splattering the walls with his blood, the boy's back erupted open. The beast had claimed another victim.

JOSH TATTON
The Kings Of Wessex Academy, Cheddar

SHADOWS

The old house that lurks at the end of the road with doors that never open and the people inside never come out, but their shadows pass the windows, showing there is life in the house. The people inside only come out when the sun has set, their skin pale like it never sees the sun and when you see their eyes it's like looking into the abyss. One night, my curiosity took control of me and I stayed up waiting until nightfall. They walked out, one man at the front, all dressed in black ready to hunt…

EMILY LOUISE EVANS (14)
The Kings Of Wessex Academy, Cheddar

OLD ENTICEMENT

The flickering of a light awakens me from my deep slumber. Sitting up, my drowsy eyes settle on the hollow doorway lying before me. The sudden crackle of thunder snaps me out of my trance. Where am I? There's a man in the doorway; his pale figure uneases me. Yet, I find myself following him through the abandoned asylum. Cold, red blood cascades from his translucent hair. Not just his complexion scares me, but the blank smile that seems plastered to his dead face. Abruptly, he stops moving, his hand rotating round in an abnormal way. 'Welcome back,' he utters.

HARRY CLUTTERBUCK
The Kings Of Wessex Academy, Cheddar

Body Swap

He'd insisted on going. After twenty years, we'd found what we thought to be his brother in a rushed grave in a misty churchyard. I'd gone to supervise, and support James.
The digger turned up early, but waited for us before breaking ground. Its large boom went to and fro between the grave and the spoil. 'Twas a freak accident. It simply hit him. It was what happened next that intrigued me. As he hit the ground, he disappeared and in his place lay the body of Jacob Morris, his murdered brother.
Then it struck me, he'd done it.

Sam Kail-Dyke (15)
The Kings Of Wessex Academy, Cheddar

The End Of The Corridor

Walking slowly down a gravelled path, I soon came across a run-down old building. Opening the door, it made a loud creak, revealing a long corridor with multiple rooms branching off, many of which had doors wide open only to reveal empty, bleak rooms. I kept walking until I reached the end of the corridor and found the one room with a closed door. Hanging on its hinges I opened it, swinging round in the wind brought in by the large open window. I walked slowly, the door slammed behind me, the next thing I knew, darkness.

Megan Agnew
The Kings Of Wessex Academy, Cheddar

UNMASKED STOP

I was waiting for the bus to take me to a Halloween party with my best pals Sami and Kyle. I sat on one of the seats the bus stop provides. Then an odd figure sat next to me, cloaked in a black robe. Then a man or a woman covered my mouth and dragged me away with a plastic knife to my throat. Was this a joke? All of a sudden the figure stood with a machete and got closer to me until he took off his hood. To my surprise it was just Sami!

CAMERON PAUL (11)
The Ridings Federation Winterbourne International Academy, Bristol

THE END...

Emily waited, the sirens screaming, the bombs blowing. The creak of the old barn house door gave her a fright. With the floorboards squealing and the damp carpet squelching, she perched against the decrepit straw wall, hoping nothing was coming her way. The centre of the brightest most colourful city had turned dark. She pulled her phone out of her muddy pocket and checked her Instagram feed. To her surprise, all that was posted was 'good luck'. Then she suddenly got loads of texts saying: 'Sorry'. Then, *boom!* Darkness...

JENNY KEMPSON (12)
The Ridings Federation Winterbourne International Academy, Bristol

THE BEDROOM

I'm on my phone, the time's 10:30pm. I'm on Facebook when I see a post saying: 'Share this in five seconds or you will die at 2:35am tomorrow'.

I go to bed and wake up at 2:30am. When I open my eyes I see the top half of a human in the doorway to my room. For the next hour I am building up the courage to turn on my lamp. Finally, I turn on my lamp and aim my handgun at the door... It is just my hoodie hanging on my door!

OWEN FREKE (13)
The Ridings Federation Winterbourne International Academy, Bristol

RESISTANCE

One by one, the rebels snuck in undetected through the back door of the dark stone castle. Up the creaky spiral stairs they climbed towards the king's throne room. Then, out of nowhere, the king and his guards surrounded the rebels to massacre them. Then, the general came to aid the rebels and cut up all the guards. The king ran away to his secret lair and took out a crystal. He used it to unleash a portal to the Underworld where all the monsters came out, spitting out fireballs which blew up the castle and the king.

JAKE FELSON (11)
The Ridings Federation Winterbourne International Academy, Bristol

THE MAN WHO ALWAYS SMILED

As darkness fell across my house, I knew it was time to head up to bed. The coldness of my house sent shivers down my spine. Suddenly, a massive bang rippled down my hallway, it had come from my bedroom. As I walked into my room, everything was normal apart from my window, it had a blood handprint on it. I slowly walked over to my window and someone was standing outside smiling at me. I closed my curtains and turned around but… there he was still smiling at me. I couldn't escape… this was the end.

BECCA ENGLAND (13)
The Ridings Federation Winterbourne International Academy, Bristol

A SLITHERING STORY

Rustle, rustle, rustle! The sound of my old Volvo was growing ever clearer in my ears. Then, *bang!* My car immediately stopped and I jumped out of my skin. Smoke enveloped my car, as I got out to see what the matter was. 'Why?' I shouted, as I realised I needed oil. Then all of a sudden… *Clatter!* 'What was that?' I said to myself and I got back in the car and locked myself in. Next there was a tap at my window and all I could see was a huge figure holding some sort of tin…

ISABELLA ROWLEY (12)
The Ridings Federation Winterbourne International Academy, Bristol

THE SPOOKY HOUSE

One dark and gloomy night in Hollywood when the power was out, Joe was alone in his house. He was so scared, he had to call his friends Archie and Rio to come for the night.

Ten minutes later they were there. Suddenly, they heard a man's voice, it sounded like a monster but they knew it wasn't. Then they heard it again, now they were scared, especially as it was getting louder. They hid under their blankets because it was extremely loud. It was still getting louder when suddenly something touched Rio's shoulder…

JOE BRAKE (11)
The Ridings Federation Winterbourne International Academy, Bristol

THE GRAVEYARD

Kara, Alex and Josh were at a graveyard on a full moon. They were playing truth or dare. Kara was the first to go. 'Truth or dare?' said Alex.

'Dare,' Kara replied.

Josh dared her to stick a knife into a grave. 'What's bad about that?' mumbled Kara.

'If you stand on a grave at night you get sucked in.'

Kara approached the grave, shivering with fear. She was on the grave. She heard strange noises. She spun around with the knife. She stabbed someone. Josh fell to his knees. 'It was only meant to be a joke,' he croaked.

FRASER JAMESON (11)
The Ridings Federation Winterbourne International Academy, Bristol

SOME FRIEND

In school on Monday, my friend, Katy, said I could go to her house. So there I was, at her house. I knocked on the door and the door slowly opened. I stepped in and the door instantly locked behind me. This felt personal.

Suddenly, a groaning sound came from a dark hallway to our left. All the lights went out. The house went silent. I made the mistake of saying, 'Hello?' What happened next was the scariest thing ever, this is why I'm writing this in my coffin. Dead. On Friday 13th. Some friend…

LAUREN BARKER (11)
The Ridings Federation Winterbourne International Academy, Bristol

THE CLOWN'S COMING!

'The sky's beautiful tonight,' Justin said. I nodded. We were lying down on a blanket in the field. Then there was a huge bang from around the block. We jumped up and ran to where the bang came from. It was an abandoned fair.

'Woah, let's go inside!' Justin said.

I ran after Justin, trying to stop him but he was too fast. Inside was full of cobwebs and ghostly rides and the Ferris wheel swinging. It was silent. Suddenly, a huge clown jumped out! It stomped around everywhere. Justin and I were terrified. I screamed and that was it.

ANGEL PITCHFORD (11)
The Ridings Federation Winterbourne International Academy, Bristol

Abandoned

It was a dark and mysterious night. Mia and Eve were strolling through the woods when they saw an abandoned hotel. It was in the middle of nowhere. The girls decided to look inside. The door was open. The girls tiptoed inside. They spotted an old wooden staircase. The stairs creaked loudly as they started to climb.

At the top of the stairs was a door, they opened it. They peered inside and saw a suitcase on the bed. They walked towards the bed, suddenly the door slammed shut behind them, both girls screamed. Eerily, a shadow appeared behind them...

Esme Fletcher (11)
The Ridings Federation Winterbourne International Academy, Bristol

The Scream

Rosie slurped the remaining hot chocolate out of her rabbit mug before she went to bed. She tried to delay by having a piece of fruit so she didn't have to go to sleep. As she was putting her mug in the dishwasher, she heard a sound that she hadn't heard before. 'Mum,' she shouted, 'there's somebody outside making weird noises.'

Her mum called her upstairs, but all of a sudden, Rosie heard a scream. A deafening scream that caused all the doors in the house to slam. Her favourite picture fell to the floor and smashed. Something was there…

Alice Primrose Irwin (11)
The Ridings Federation Winterbourne International Academy, Bristol

A Ghost In The House

One day after my son got home from work, he cooked us some food, then we sat down in the lounge and we ate it. Out of the corner of my eye I could see strange shadows going up the stairs through the window in the door. When I looked up they were gone, this happened a few times.

After a few nights something horrible happened to me, I felt a breath on my cheek so I called out, 'Who's there?' No reply. I tried to get to sleep but then I felt something touch my arm…

JOSH NEWLAND (11)
The Ridings Federation Winterbourne International Academy, Bristol

The Figure

Running and panting, Steve found an abandoned mansion next to the main road. He ran in and shouted, 'Hello, anyone home?' No answer! He walked into the kitchen and everything moved from cookers turning on, to knives flying at him. He ran to the lounge where the fire was burning and the furniture was getting lifted up and thrown across the room! Steve saw a white figure in the doorway but then it walked away silently. Steve ran to the front door which closed and locked. He couldn't get out. The figure approached, the room was silent…

CHARLIE CHURCH (11)
The Ridings Federation Winterbourne International Academy, Bristol

THE VIOLIN OF DEATH

I heard that scary, disturbing noise again. I realised it was coming from the basement.
I made my way to the basement door, slowly walking down the dark staircase with only the dim light of the hallway. I was scared, the noise was getting louder. I had goosebumps, but kept going.
My heart was beating so hard. I stepped into the middle of the basement. I saw the noise was coming from an old violin playing by itself. The noise grew louder and I felt myself become mesmerised. I fell into a trance, a trance that led to death.

OLIVER DAVID HENRY TUBEY (11)
The Ridings Federation Winterbourne International Academy, Bristol

THE HORROR OF THE SLENDER-MAN

One ordinary school night, a girl named Dannie arose to the truly horrifying sight of the Slender Man. She glanced to the left to see a white face and the glimpse of a brand new suit peering into her second floor window, but there was no ladder, his legs touched the ground! Her eyes started to bulge inwards into darkness as streams of blood started shooting down her face. Dannie's black hair turned curly and rotten. Her white pyjamas became bloody, then she let out a high-pitched scream of death into the night! Slender Man evilly laughed!

ALBIE REES (11)
The Ridings Federation Winterbourne International Academy, Bristol

Amy

We were at Morfa Bay for Year 6 camp. I shared a cabin with my three friends: Islay, Harriette and Amy. It was our second night of being there and I was heading to bed. I walked in and saw Amy's long blonde hair dangling from the bed. I climbed up to my bed and closed my eyes. Suddenly, I heard the hinges creak. I looked at the door, there was a figure. I looked up and standing in front of me was… Amy.

ELLA CARTER (11)
The Ridings Federation Winterbourne International Academy, Bristol

Deafening Scream

It was at least 10 years go when a young boy was playing in the fields when he was on his way home. He passed a house which his mum said had been empty for at least 50 years. Then he had an amazing idea, he was going to show his friends that he was brave. It was five to twelve as he walked in. He walked up the rotten stairs, then there was a loud bang, it sounded like the door was closing. Then there was a deafening scream…

HAYDEN THOMPSON (11)
The Ridings Federation Winterbourne International Academy, Bristol

One Bad Holiday

'What a great day to go sailing,' said Greg. It was the summer holidays and Greg and John were relaxing in the sun, everything was silent.
Suddenly, they noticed that a dead man was floating in the water. Scared to death, Greg steered the boat around but John fell overboard. John couldn't swim, however Greg could, so he dived down to save his friend. Once under the water, the floating corpse in the water transformed into a great white shark which breathed fire, killing both of them.

TOBY LANE (11)
The Ridings Federation Winterbourne International Academy, Bristol

The Tic Tac Spatula Clown

The sound of my clock bounced around my room. I thought I was alone, but I wasn't… My bed shook and I felt a hand graze my shoulder, I turned around. My head throbbed and my heart beat madly as I saw the terrible face of the clown, it was the one ticking! I couldn't even begin to imagine what was behind its terrible mask… Then I noticed my bear was gone, and with its crooked hands, the clown was grasping it. I couldn't look as a blade shot out of its arm, for I knew it was me next…

ZOE BEALE (11)
The Ridings Federation Winterbourne International Academy, Bristol

Towels Of Death!

2006… the early morning scare…
I woke up at 3:02am and I peered around my room until I saw a figure which looked similar to a human being. I felt a chill down my spine. I slid down and tucked myself into the quilt. I began to cry. Later that night, my mum came running into my room to see if I was OK. I said there was somebody standing over in the corner, however when she turned on the light, it was just a bunch of towels stacked on top of each other!

Owen Barry James Brain (11)
The Ridings Federation Winterbourne International Academy, Bristol

Halloween Night

It was October 31st. I was out alone, trick or treating, getting candy. It was fun, I had a flashlight and a basket full of candy. I was 25 minutes away from home. It was 11 o'clock at night and the wind blew the leaves around. I wondered whether to call it a night or get more candy. I decided to go home, but knocked on doors on the way.
I made it to my road. I saw the shadow of a man. I didn't recognise him so I walked on, but when I looked around it was too late…

Charlotte Pleass (11)
The Ridings Federation Winterbourne International Academy, Bristol

THE MAN

'Lily run!'
That night was the scariest night of my life. It was a gloomy night,
Lily and I were in my rubbish, old, dusty Volkswagen driving around
at about 11:30 listening to James Blunt classics! At that time we
were both getting scared so I turned the music loud and was singing
away, when out of the blue something hit the car! We ran out worried,
but no damage was done to the car. I looked under the car to see
what we hit. I was shocked. It was laughing. I got up and Lily was
gone…

ARCHIE CROUCHER (11)
The Ridings Federation Winterbourne International Academy, Bristol

DREAM CATCHER

I decided to make the brave decision to go travelling in the gloomy,
some say, 'haunted woods'. I had been walking for hours on end
and suddenly tripped over a rock, I stumbled back up to my jelly-like
feet and stared at the rock. It went! I couldn't believe my eyes, it was
there and it was like it magically disappeared. Something jumped
on me! It was a hairy, slimy creature. I couldn't remember much after
that. I woke up in a shadowy corridor, there was no one else to be
seen except me…

LIBBY WILLIAMS (12)
The Ridings Federation Winterbourne International Academy, Bristol

Worse Than Death...

She ran. She didn't know what from or what to. She turned a corner and a hooded figure was there. She kept on running. She turned another corner, but it was there again. She kept on running and running but she couldn't get away from it. She got trapped in a corner. There was no way out. The figure stood there. It reached for its hood and pulled it off. Its face was just a small hole. It grabbed her and sucked out her soul.
Beware, it's still there and looking for new victims. The end... for now...

Luke Goad (12)
The Ridings Federation Winterbourne International Academy, Bristol

Mail

Walking through the old, gloomy forest, I swept past an old, abandoned house. I was sure that if I screamed no one would hear. I had the sudden urge to enter the house: like, it was calling out to me. Entering the house slowly, the wind slammed the door behind me. I strolled upstairs to the front of a bedroom: to meet a shadowy man at the corner. The man crept towards me with his long legs. He pulled up a knife and cut me! Apparently a carcass was found days afterwards on my doorstep with a note reading: 'Mail'.

Desola Idisha (13)
The Ridings Federation Winterbourne International Academy, Bristol

THE DEMON THAT FELL IN LOVE...

Lizzy and I had an after-school detention, so when we finished our lessons, we made our way up to the top floor and sat down in our sixth period classroom to read. All of a sudden, a red glow flooded the room, it was him, the demon! He floated towards us, it was terrifying! Horrified, he looked me in the eyes and spoke these words, 'Please will you marry me and you will get everything you desire! If you say yes, we can rule this desolate world together and it will be perfect... '

MARTHA FRANCES DERRICK (13)
The Ridings Federation Winterbourne International Academy, Bristol

THE DARK MYSTERY

Awake, I was awake in a dark, dusty corridor. After waiting for a few minutes for my eyes to get used to the dark, I walked down the corridor towards the old, rotting door and I slowly opened it. *Creak!* Into the room I went. Hanging from the ceiling was a dead, rotting person, tied from a rope in the middle of the room. Blank. My mind was blank and I was afraid. Then I ran out the door and tripped over a bed. Then *whoosh!* A bird flew in and carried me away! The nightmare was over…

ALEX WARE (11)
The Ridings Federation Winterbourne International Academy, Bristol

THE UNEXPECTED VISITOR

Molly and I were sat watching TV alone yesterday. Something didn't feel right, it didn't feel like we were alone. Then, above us, I heard a noise. It was like someone was creeping around upstairs. Molly seemed to hear it too because she agreed to come and look upstairs with me. Things weren't right. Doors were open and my bed sheets were rumpled. *Bang!* A loud noise came from my sister's room. We both crept in. Nothing there. We checked under the bed. I leapt back, two cold eyes were staring at us…

MILLIE WILLS (11)
The Ridings Federation Winterbourne International Academy, Bristol

HELP

It was coming, they could see it now. People were screaming, crying, helpless! Moving closer by the second, the whole city scrambled up buildings, people ran for their lives. The wind was strong, the sky was a blanket of dark black. It was happening, most people struggled to believe it. It could be the end for everyone!
It had reached the beach. Everyone was bracing themselves for it, for when it hit, for when it crashed down on everything. Then it was here, it just touched the building and took it down. Everyone was going to die. It was here!

KIAN GOODWIN (11)
The Ridings Federation Winterbourne International Academy, Bristol

THE ZOMBIE APOCALYPSE

It all started with a deathly scream. I was asleep, at 11:30pm. I woke up. Something was wrong. I could feel it. I climbed out of bed and tiptoed downstairs. I heard snarling, chilling me to the bone. I didn't want to find out what it was, but I couldn't turn back. I was in the kitchen, and what I saw made me vomit. Something was crouched over my parents, eating. It had mouldy green skin and half of its arm had been ripped off by razor-sharp teeth. The figure turned and stared at me. Zombies…

ADAM VORAJEE (11)
The Ridings Federation Winterbourne International Academy, Bristol

THE OFFICE

It was Halloween. Lewis was about to leave the office. Suddenly, he heard a blood-curdling scream. He grabbed his phone and ran down the corridor. The lights started to flicker. 'Hello, anyone there?' A small whimper coming from Simon's office. Lewis opened the door. Simon was under his desk cuddling a Corgi teddy. They walked down to the main room. Everything was pitch-black. Shadows crept towards them. It got clearer that it wasn't a monster, it was Sips, Hannah and Kim! Later on Lewis saw a video on Sips' YouTube channel, it was them reacting to that night.

CHLOE DAVIES (14)
The Ridings Federation Winterbourne International Academy, Bristol

My Story

Rain hits the window, the wipers drag it against the dirty windshield. The kids are yelling in the back of the car and complaining that they're cold. Then the radio silences and the gate opens. When they approach the wooden lodge, dressed with snow, the door creaks open and they walk in. Still cold, the kids ask if they can light the fire. The man leaves to get some firewood. As he approaches the shed, a strong wind picks up. He runs from the shed but something moves in the leaves. A strange figure appears. The screams are silenced.

CHARLIE HOOPER (13)
The Ridings Federation Winterbourne International Academy, Bristol

The Haunted Overnight Stay

I was at a sleepover. We were in our sleeping bags eating sweets. Then we started to hear a noise in the middle of the night and we saw a shadow coming towards the room. We were so scared, then we heard bangs like footsteps coming towards us. The radiators started to rumble. Suddenly, it came closer and closer. All of us hid away but my friend and I got out of bed to see what the noise was... Phew! It was just Eloise's dad coming to see if we were asleep.

KALI BUFFERY (11)
The Ridings Federation Winterbourne International Academy, Bristol

THE UNEXPECTED FIGURE

Bobby was having a sleepover at his house with his best friend Kobe and some other friends. It was around 11:30 and it was pitch-black when Bobby got up to go to the toilet. Suddenly, Kobe and his friends heard a loud, spooky sound and it was coming towards them. The door opened slowly and a white figure emerged. It slowly crept towards Kobe whilst he was moving backwards into the wall at every second. The figure got within a foot of Kobe and shouted, 'Boooooo!' It was Bobby with a white sheet on him. Everybody laughed, even Kobe.

CALLUM LONG (13)
The Ridings Federation Winterbourne International Academy, Bristol

PIERCING PAIN

The dead trees were whistling in the wind, while rain fell out of the dull grey sky, giving the church a strange aura. As the sound of the glass gravestones breaking went through my ears, I heard a tone-deaf crow screeching loudly, piercing the silent atmosphere. Creaking every so often, the wooden panelled door kept on slamming itself shut, creating a bellowing sound circling the church. As the lightning struck onto the glass windows, shattering every one of them, dust and fog surrounded the dark figure and the noise was piercing painfully through my ears.

CASEY JASMINE VERRINDER (13)
The Ridings Federation Winterbourne International Academy, Bristol

The Dolly Girl!

A house was dark and deserted, apart from a five-year-old girl who had the face of a doll. The outside world thought that she was vulnerable. When her back was turned something or someone dropped down from behind her. It was a male, aged around 17, who said in a frightened voice, 'Are you OK little girl?' As he said this, the girl slowly rotated. She pounced at the male with ease but full of anger and he disintegrated within seconds. She laughed vigorously as she moved on to her next victim.

JEREMY YEARSLEY (13)
The Ridings Federation Winterbourne International Academy, Bristol

The Figure

Jim was a reporter who was going to a church. A thick mist covered the church so it was barely viewable. The gate squeaked as Jim walked through. As Jim slowly crept to the front door, lightning struck the church, causing a pillar to collapse. The door creaked as he walked in. As he got further into the giant hall, the floorboards broke, leaving Jim in the basement with a broken ankle. At that moment, Jim realised he was in an asylum with exploded guts and blood splattered all over the wall. That was when he noticed he wasn't alone…

SHANE EDSER (13)
The Ridings Federation Winterbourne International Academy, Bristol

THE LANE

Me and my friend were walking down a lane. I hate lanes anyway so I did not want to go down but if we went around the lane, it was miles out of our way to get to the shop. We were discussing if we should go down it or not, but like the idiots we are, we decided to go down it so we did. I heard a rustling in the trees. I thought it was a bird and then we heard a voice and it said, 'Get out of my lane!'

RIO STEPHEN TEMPLAR (11)
The Ridings Federation Winterbourne International Academy, Bristol

THE ALLEY

It was a gloomy, stormy night, when my friend and I went down a dilapidated, old, creepy alleyway where darkness consumed all. As we carried on walking (not knowing what was to come) a leg out of nowhere swooped across and took us out! We scraped to our knees and with one huge jump my friend and I sprinted as fast as we could. Then a strange figure stopped us in our tracks, he said, 'Hello boys! Ha, ha, ha!' We tried to escape but his muscular arms grabbed us, that is all I remember…

MATTHEW MILLARD (11)
The Ridings Federation Winterbourne International Academy, Bristol

MIDNIGHT DREAMS

The clock struck 12. The wind violently ripped through the trees, breaking everything in its path. Walking through the deserted forest, nothing moved, not a sound. Emily checked her every move. Turning and twisting, trying not to break a branch on the floor, she was unaware of being watched. Emily felt like she had been walking for hours but actually only 25 minutes had passed, but then she heard a voice whisper her name. Then again but louder. It carried on until she suddenly saw someone walking towards her. Suddenly, she woke up and realised it was happening, happening again…

CHLOE SNOOK (14)
The Ridings Federation Winterbourne International Academy, Bristol

THE SHADOW

One dark, gloomy Halloween night, three boys were coming back from a party at midnight. They stumbled across a forest, it was the only way to get home so they went in. The leaves rattled and they heard a scream so they ran but they got split up and poor James was all alone. He saw a shadow but within a split second it was gone. *Snap!* He shouted, 'Who's there?' No one replied so he sprinted in fear but he fell on the cold, hard ground. A mysterious shadow dragged him into the darkness. He was never seen again.

HARRY DURNELL (11)
The Ridings Federation Winterbourne International Academy, Bristol

THE HORROR

Justin and I walked into the forest because it started to rain! In the forest we both decided to sit on a wet log. It was getting darker by the minute. Then it happened... A monstrous beast came. We heard the footsteps getting closer and faster... We both tried to outrun it, but it was no use. Then it caught up with us and jumped...
It was just a little squirrel!

HARVEY DRAKE (11)
The Ridings Federation Winterbourne International Academy, Bristol

THE STRANGE NIGHT

I went into my bedroom and got ready for bed. When I finished getting ready I jumped into bed and as soon as I got into my bed there was a strange light coming from outside. At that moment I was so scared I didn't even want to look out, but I did. There was a shadow like a creature trying to eat my plants in my garden and then my security light came on and the creature ran away! I realised it was a cat that one of my neighbours had let out!

MOLLY ROSE HODGE (13)
The Ridings Federation Winterbourne International Academy, Bristol

FALLING, DEAD, ALIVE

I once knew a girl called Catherine, we were best friends, we did everything together and on her 7th birthday a theme park came to town. Some said it was haunted but it became more intriguing. We climbed to the top of the highest ride. It was beautiful but then she lost her balance. I tried to help, but it wasn't enough, she died and it was all my fault. I'm 18 now and I'm moving into my new house, not far from the graveyard.

After settling in, there was a knock at the door, it was Catherine…

NICOLE GOLDING (14)
The Ridings Federation Winterbourne International Academy, Bristol

ONE NIGHT…

One night I was awoken by the sound of rustling. First I didn't think much, I just thought it would be my dog, so I just fell back to sleep. One night, the next week, I heard the same noise, but this time I was petrified. I grabbed the BB gun from my bedside cabinet, I was just about to open the door then I heard the noise again. I picked up a glass bottle, then went downstairs. There were pig-headed humans everywhere, one of them slit my throat…

Then the alarm went off and I woke up.

GEORGE PEARCE (13)
The Ridings Federation Winterbourne International Academy, Bristol

THE TALE OF DEVILMAN

The man walked slowly into the down-town church. It was dark and foggy with moonlight just shining through the gloom. His red eyes glinted as he stared at the cross on the altar. The feelings started to well up inside him all over again - he wanted to kill someone! He clenched his fist and plunged it into the font of holy water. Steam rose and he screamed as his hand burnt in the now boiling water! His head spun round and he fixed his gaze on the cross which burst into flames - leaving a pile of ash on the floor...

HAYDEN-LEE SCARROTT
Voyage Learning Campus, Bristol

SPOOKY CHRISTMAS

It was a gloomy, foggy night. Michael hadn't been very good this year. His dad would always say Santa wouldn't bring him presents if he wasn't good. Michael thought Santa would bring presents no matter what. It was Christmas Eve and Michael fell asleep with thoughts of Santa and the presents he would receive. Michael awoke with a cold chill and a shiver down his PJs. His door creaked open slowly and a red light shone from downstairs. He walked downstairs thinking it was Santa but it wasn't! A sharp turn and in front a man with horns...

KYLE BURNLEY (13)
Voyage Learning Campus, Bristol

ANNABELLE

The fog was blooming through the letterbox. Jason crept down the stairs and, in the chair at the bottom of the stairs, sat a doll called Annabelle. With her dark red eyes she stared and screeched a giggle. Jason's heart pounded and he could feel it hit his chest as cold sweat dipped like a waterfall from his head. He ran into each and every room but the shadows followed him along the dark, dusty and cold walls. Annabelle suddenly appeared behind him. Grabbing him at his ankles and pulling him down to the soggy, wet, dirty cellar...

LIAM WHITE (13)
Voyage Learning Campus, Bristol

THE WALK I NEVER CAME BACK FROM

I was walking down the abandoned road. The houses either side creaked in the mist. Quickening my pace, I turned rapidly around the corner.

A dark figure in the mist stood before me. A scream of terror roared through my throat.

As the figure approached me my whole body shook in fear. My eyes darted around looking for an escape. The dark figure reached out to grab me, but I stumbled back and dashed to the nearest house.

Bang! Bang! on the door. I cowered in fear. The door burst open. I squealed.

It had found me...

JACOB ASHDOWN (11)
Voyage Learning Campus, Bristol

The Night I Didn't Live

On a dark, foggy night I went looking for Dracula's mansion.
Suddenly, out of the fog, appeared a great metal gate. I went deep
into the dying mansion. I found a sword made of silver and jewels. I
held it tight in my hand whilst trying to keep my eyes open. I couldn't
resist, I closed then opened them. A dark figure appeared in the air. I
was paralysed, couldn't move, couldn't breathe.
He walked up to me and asked with a deep dying voice, 'Do you fear
death?' He reached for my neck then... I woke up covered in sweat.

Gabriel Budasz (15)
Voyage Learning Campus - Weston, Oldmixon

Are You Lost?

It was finally the 13th in my cold, uninteresting apartment. Pictures
were shaking furiously, making me want to scream so it would just
go away. Then a silhouette of a young child appeared in my kitchen
singing, 'Hello,I'm coming for you!'
The hairs stood straight up all over my body. Was I seeing things?
Am I insane? Every day more and more people appeared, it was like
a family reunion. One day a young gentleman ran his hand across
my hand. My heart stopped. All went quiet... from that dream I was
never the same. My life changed completely.

Hannah Pratt (14)
Worle Community School, Weston-Super-Mare

ABANDONED

Quietness. I've never seen a town so abandoned. Where had everyone gone. My parents! Gone. All alone, nothing to do. I felt myself panicking. Rain poured down. I heard loud noises. Smashed windows. Glass everywhere. Didn't know what to do! Where to go! Walking down the streets, dripping wet. *Crash!* What was that? I thought it was abandoned. Holding my breath, heart pounding hard, I ran to the safehold. I sat on the floor, tears dripping down my face. The safehold windows smashed! *Bang! Bang!* Something out there... The door swung hard open! What should I do?

NICOLE ENGLISH (14)
Worle Community School, Weston-Super-Mare

THE VAMPIRE

I looked up at the glistening moon. It looked like a diamond. I walked up to the house and looked around. My legs shaking, my palms sweating. What was this place?
Suddenly, there was a smash. I jumped and turned around. There wasn't anything there. Then I spotted glass. There were bloodstains. I was not alone. The curtains were blowing in the wind creating a creepy whistling sound. A black shadow suddenly emerged. The shape of a person. The person was getting closer and closer. I saw teeth and a pale face. That was the last thing I saw.

LUCY HARTSHORN
Worle Community School, Weston-Super-Mare

The Big Black Hole

I swear this wasn't here before. I walk past here every day on the way to school. It's never been here. I look around with my torch, because it's dark, to see if anyone's around. I want to see what's inside but I don't know how I'll get out. I probably should just go home, but I'm curious. I lie down on the dirty floor and press my head on the side. I hear noises, drowning, deep noises. A cold chill runs through my body. I stand and my foot slips. I fall inside and can't leave...

Yasmin Luffman (13)
Worle Community School, Weston-Super-Mare

Lethal Game

Running. I hate running. If I wasn't being chased then I wouldn't. The growling behind me became clearer with every step. I hid behind a tree and it ran forward. Assembling my gun, I ran to the house. Pacing up and down, I started to panic. It seemed hunting werewolves was hard enough. Suddenly, something grabbed me and I was pulled out of the window. My breath escaped me. Its claws dug into me. I tried to get away but it was no good. It threw me into a ditch. It was no use. I was trapped...

Elesha-May Faith Smith (14)
Worle Community School, Weston-Super-Mare

UNTITLED

I woke up to the sound of dripping water.
I felt a breath on my face. Opening my eyes I finally saw what had happened.
I'd been kidnapped but by no ordinary kidnappers. Blood on their lips, sharp, shiny teeth drenched in blood and flesh.
Thoughts raced through my mind, *is this the end?*
I let out a great scream as one of them sank their teeth into my arm.
The feast had begun and I was the main course.
Gathering, all of them now, without warning, lunged forward and proceeded to feast upon my soft, fatty flesh!

MATTHEW GOODWIN (13)
Worle Community School, Weston-Super-Mare

UNTITLED

The night was slowly creeping in. An old, abandoned house appeared in the distance. With a tremble from my foot and a pound from my heart, I gradually forced my body closer. The strong wind blew up my spine. I aggressively shivered. I pushed open the rusty and creaky gate as a drop of rain poured down my face. A figure stood in front of me; I froze. I stuttered, 'Hello... Anyone there?' Two red eyes pierced into mine. I slowly shuffled backwards. I tripped over what felt like a stone and quickly yelped as the figure grabbed me...

DAISY STEELE (14)
Worle Community School, Weston-Super-Mare

THE MIDNIGHT WALKER

I slowly made my way down the street. The street lights flashing off one by one. The last light went out. A cold breeze swept down the street and brushed against my face. A flash out of the corner of my eye. The thud of footsteps behind me. My heart jumped out of my chest. I took a step to run but was stopped in my tracks by an ice-cold hand cradling my neck. I closed my eyes, not wanting to see the creature that was holding onto me. Teeth in flesh was the last thing I remembered.

LYDIA CASHMORE (13)
Worle Community School, Weston-Super-Mare

THE FIGURE IN THE DARK

You walk down the street when your phone rings. A dark voice tells you to go home now. You are scared but keep walking. A storm is coming in. Suddenly lightning strikes behind you. A figure appears. You start running. Your house is not far but you duck into an old house. Clouds cover it. You need to get home. This makes you scared! As you get up to leave, you see him. Darting out, he sees you. You run, faster and faster. Suddenly you trip! A warm hand touches you. Wondering what's happened, you get taken away. You disappear...

JOSHUA CLAY (13)
Worle Community School, Weston-Super-Mare

THE ID

The man was being dragged along the dark, disgusting mud, his eyes watched me the whole way there. The trees' eyes watched me. If it was the right thing to do, I didn't know. Dragging along the mossy, disgusting corpse, the fog grew thicker. I stumbled across the graveyard. I kicked the door open, the door screamed. I heard the rotted graves saying, 'Not again.' I started digging the hole. Every time I looked back at the corpse his eyes watched me. I chucked him in. I started to shovel the soggy mud back in the hole. My death approached...

JACK LEES (13)
Worle Community School, Weston-Super-Mare

THE BLACK-EYED CHILD

A slow, echoing knock. I opened the door. A little girl, her jumper hood hiding her face, asked if I wanted to buy a magazine. She wasn't holding any. I asked why. She said she wanted to come in. I asked why. Muffled by her hood, she said it again. I refused. Again! The door was starting to creak open. My arm was moving it; it wasn't me. I shouted no! I Tried to slam the door. She stopped it. She slid off her hood. I saw. Her eyes were black. Completely. It was a good magazine...

PHOENIX HARRIS (13)
Worle Community School, Weston-Super-Mare

James And Terry's Adventures: Kino Der Toten

James and Terry ran to the door. They heard the dogs barking. They were very worried. As they broke the door down the dogs were very close. They got into the teleporter and arrived at the bedroom. It was cold and dark. Suddenly, they left. They were back at the teleporter. They had bought themselves some time. They started running but before long, something bit into Terry's leg. He shouted for help but James couldn't go back. He got out in tears, leaving Terry behind. James was sure, for now, the dogs caught Terry and Terry was dead...

CALLUM SMETHEM (13)
Worle Community School, Weston-Super-Mare

Tomorrow Is Another Day

It's hard being bullied. Well, was hard. They were always calling me names. That's why I left. Although I miss my parents, it was the right choice. It's not so bad, I can be anywhere I want to be. The names are still with me. There are always weird things happening, noises, ghosts, all paranormal. I always connect with them. I enjoy the unseen beings, never knowing whether they are real. The bullies made me leave, the paranormal accept me. The bullies can't get me now. Now that I am dead! That's not a bother. Tomorrow is another day.

MATTHEW MOORE (14)
Worle Community School, Weston-Super-Mare

THE TRAGIC DEATH OF ZAK

There was a boy called Zak. He lived with his nan in a creepy wood.
Every night Zak heard strange noises. One night, he heard the same
noise, so he sat up and listened. It said, 'Come outside Zak. Follow
me Zak!'
So Zak went out and was attacked by what he suspected was a
wolf. He fainted and woke up in a cottage. He looked around and
saw his nan. He cried, 'Nan, Nan!' She ignored him. Then he heard a
crackling noise and he fell into a blazing fire... He died!

KIERAN KEITH JOHN BURROUGH (14)
Worle Community School, Weston-Super-Mare

TOWN OF DARKNESS

Once, a boy was on lookout duty for the town for werewolves and
vampires.
One day, the boy pretended to see a werewolf. The town came out
with guns. They found out it was a hoax and just a deer.
The next night he pretended to see a vampire. Again they came
running with guns. Turned out it was just a farmer.
The next night he heard claws and howling. He lost the feeling in his
arm. There was a vampire and werewolf attacking him. He cried out
but no one heard him scream...

JAKE JONES (13)
Worle Community School, Weston-Super-Mare

THE FOREST

In a dark forest a little cottage lies. In that cottage lived a family of three. The girl had a curfew to be back home at sunset. Her parents told her that after sunset wolves hunted. One day, the girl thought that it was a lie because she had looked out her window at night but saw nothing. She decided to take her time going home. The pale moon was at its highest. She heard howling. Something bit her arm. As pain rushed through her, she looked up to the shining full moon and everything went black.

YASMIN REBECCA WEST (13)
Worle Community School, Weston-Super-Mare

BLOODSTAINED COAT

I was in the woods, running for my life. I came across an old, abandoned house, that looked wrecked and damaged. There were smashed windows, creaking floorboards and it smelt like rotting flesh. I started to look around to see if there were any lifeless bodies but all I found was a white bloodstained shirt that was ripped the whole way through. I saw a face in the window. I followed it into the house. It wasn't there but there were loud bangs. Then there was a *tap, tap, tap* and then an old, dead, white hand held me tight...

LOTTIE LEWIS (13)
Worle Community School, Weston-Super-Mare

UNTITLED

The gates opened slowly as the sun disappeared. A trail leading into the deep, dark forest. The frightful thoughts of his childhood came rushing back to him. He took a few steps and he was already hearing things. A shadow which didn't belong to him was to his left but just before he turned to look, it was gone... It started to drizzle with rain. He pulled a knife out of his pocket as he heard the trees creak and saw a sudden movement. He threw the knife and someone fell. The screech was as loud as the thunder.

BEN GRIFFITH (13)
Worle Community School, Weston-Super-Mare

THERE'S SOMEONE IN THE CUPBOARD

It was the middle of the night when suddenly my cupboard door opened slowly. I jumped straight up and huddled in the corner. I heard a scratching sound from above. I cautiously looked up; nothing. I buried my head in my hands and whispered, 'Not again. Please not again.'
As I lifted my head, a voice echoed around the room, 'Hello Clarisse.' I tried to figure out where it was coming from, but to no avail. I peered into the darkness as two scrawny fingers appeared at the end of my bed. I told Mum there was someone in there...

MEGAN WILLIAMS (14)
Worle Community School, Weston-Super-Mare

The Incredible ID!

Starting off my day with a joyful feeling. Sunny outside, which made me happy. It was 11:55am, watching the minutes tick by. At exactly 12pm it started raining, which made me feel down. Suddenly, my stomach felt like someone was angry, punching my stomach. Shaking like a leaf, I suddenly thought... *it's the ID trying to escape!* The pain started to get even more painful. I blinked, sat on the sofa, I looked at where the inside creature was punching...

BETH SHERIDAN (13)
Worle Community School, Weston-Super-Mare

The Graveyard

As I stepped into the abandoned graveyard I felt a pulling at my feet. I looked down, there was nothing there. I went to visit my child's grave when I heard a voice. 'Daddy!' it said. I jumped and hoped to see my little girl but all I saw were two eyes looking at me from the darkness and a crow perched on a grave. A hand grabbed me from the darkness and pulled me in, like a boy on Halloween and I saw the pale face... It was me! I turned around, read the grave, it said: 'Jack'.

FABIAN MULDOON (13)
Worle Community School, Weston-Super-Mare

ME IN THE MIRROR

I crept closer and closer to the sharp, shattered mirror in the corner of my enclosing master bedroom, waiting to see whether he had returned. When I stood in front of the mirror of my nightmares, his eyes burned into my soul. His skin had turned into a more prominent yellow and his eyes black as the midnight sky. I turned around swiftly trying to escape myself, but when I did I saw myself staring back at me. We both froze, stuck to the rotten floorboards beneath me. I couldn't escape me, my hatred grew bigger for me every day.

AMY DOBSON (13)
Worle Community School, Weston-Super-Mare

MY REFLECTION

I stepped in front of the mirror. I noticed a strange look in the eyes of my reflection. Possessing a fiery, demonic appearance. The smile on his face, far from heartwarming. A knife was held high in his hand. His hand raised, as did mine. The knife gripped tightly. The look he gave me. I knew what was coming next. I bit my lip hard. Trying to distract myself from all the pain I began to black out as blood rushed out of me. The reflection returned with that same heartless grin. I opened my eyes... in a mental asylum.

THOMAS LIGHTOWLER (13)
Worle Community School, Weston-Super-Mare

To My Hiding Place

The night the madman escaped, twelve people died. Twelve souls ricochet off the cobbled clouds, looking for someone to haunt; someone - anyone - to blame for their deaths. Three chose asylum guards, four chose locksmiths, three chose authorities and one chose the madman's crippled elderly mother. The final one still wanders looking for her killer. She will never find me - hidden in plain sight. Not hidden in your sagging, boneless skin.

MAISIE SLINGSBY (13)
Worle Community School, Weston-Super-Mare

Becoming A Doll

Scratched knees smeared blood on the stone as she crawled through the gap that led to light. Breathing heavily, eyes searched through dust-covered relics as candles lit up the damp stone chamber, not noticing dolls twitching. Suddenly, china hands grabbed her raven locks while shadows covered her enlarged azure eyes. Flickering candles died out, leaving a smoky smell that smothered her senses as she thrashed in constricting limbs. Silence settled in the black abyss... Candles lit up the chamber, revealing her china body limp on the floor. Her eyes opened to see dolls surrounding her. Dolls, just like herself...

LEXI MITCHELL (13)
Worle Community School, Weston-Super-Mare

WHO ARE YOU? OR WHAT?

Exploring the forest had seemed like a thrilling idea while it was daylight, but now I had different ideas. The moonlight had begun to fade heavily just leaving the sight of fog eerily rolling in. There was no chance I could find my way out in this darkness and I knew my parents would be worried. *Let's text them,* I thought. No service... great. Panicked, I began to run. *Thud!* I lay motionless on the gritty, undulating ground. A face appeared and helped me up. Who was it? Or what? 'Who are you... or what?' I asked.
No answer...

LIBBY MOORE (14)
Worle Community School, Weston-Super-Mare

THE FOREST

The forest set ablaze with red-hot fire. Crows dispersed from their nests like children scatter when their parents call for them. Justin tried to follow them, but his way was blocked by the inferno. He concluded that his best bet was to take shelter inside the rickety house. The decaying door was held on by a single aged and rusty hinge. Mould and moss covered the ramshackle walls of the building, The furniture inside the house was all broken, missing legs and other serious pieces. The nearest village was over fifty miles away. He was a lost child. Forever.

KRISZTIAN KORMOS (13)
Worle Community School, Weston-Super-Mare

THE PIECES

I kept a careful eye as he charged through the laundry room door. Desperation raging, he tore through piles of old toys until he found a blank white box. Opening it led to the revelation of a jigsaw, plain white with sets of initials on certain pieces. Gazing upon it, he turned deathly pale and slumped forwards, now inanimate. My eyes drew towards it as his initials were engraved into another piece of the puzzle. At that very moment, I knew I was next... Immediately, I bolted for the exit, but it was too late... A piece in the puzzle.

JORDAN ANDREWS (14)
Worle Community School, Weston-Super-Mare

THE SHADOW

A dark shadow crept upon the chilling castle. Fog rose over the doorway. It was locked. No way to escape; all doors were locked. The shadow grew greater. What was it? My heart raced. I tried once again to open the locked door. What could I do? It was as if I was running from my death. Time was rapidly running out for me...

MOLLY O'FLAHERTY (14)
Worle Community School, Weston-Super-Mare

THE WHISPERER

Stalagmites littered the floor like the teeth of a lion. The pungent smell of sulphur lingered in the cave. The trio edged deeper into the rocky slumber, not thinking about their return. Soft whispers poisoned their ears with rumours and alien sounds. They grew louder and louder. Nothing could stop the piercing melodies.

'Argh!' Lauren let out a hellish scream that echoed in the cave.

'Lauren? Lauren, where are you?' Brandon cried. Two cold hands latched onto Brandon's skinny, skinny ankles. He was dragged into darkness.

Chris moved gingerly, not knowing what to expect.

'We are behind you Chris... '

TOM DERRICK (13)
Worle Community School, Weston-Super-Mare

The Enticing Sound

The hollow sound of emotionless music bled through the empty streets. I heard the noise and began to follow; I found the house, it was an empty shell devoid of compassion, once filled with life. Thunder cackled in the sky, sensing my dread. I cautiously entered through the door set ajar. The wooden hallway I passed through was like the artery of the heart of my curiosity. Slowly moving my feet, time seemed to stop. My heart relaxed. My brain felt on edge. In the bare room, the gramophone scratched. I gingerly elevated the needle. There was a click...

Archie Jones (13)
Worle Community School, Weston-Super-Mare

The Path

The path stretched out for miles, lit by only one flickering street light. Suddenly, in the light, I saw a figure, it was gone in a split second. My skin crawled, my heart raced and I found it hard to breathe.
All of a sudden, I noticed a run-down house in the distance and it had a large amount of ivy growing up the walls and broken-in windows. Then the figure appeared again. I saw that it was a pale child with awful bleeding eyes and cruel, unforgiving looks. Then she opened her mouth and smiled...

Zack Wigmore (13)
Worle Community School, Weston-Super-Mare

A Night At Transylvania

I was outside the castle foraging for food, when I heard a distant rumble. I ran inside. I heard the door creak and a small thin person walked in. He looked around and spotted me in the corner. I tried to get away but he found me. He reached into his pocket and... *Zzzz* I woke up and was surrounded by knives and dangerous-looking tools. He walked over to me and grabbed a knife. He went to my head and *bam!* He cut it clean off. Unknown to him I could still see. My revenge would be sweet...

FRASER POCOCK (13)
Worle Community School, Weston-Super-Mare

The Figure Under My Bed

It was the darkest, most frightening hour of the night, I could hear eerie sounds coming from under my bed. They howled my name over and over again. As I got up I saw something ghostly and humanoid move across like the speed of sound to the end of my room. I quickly glared at it. However it wasn't there. I turned my head and rolled over. As my rage increased at the voices in my head I... I couldn't take it anymore. This time it was over. I was really mad. The figure reached out for me and snatched...

HARRY PENN (14)
Worle Community School, Weston-Super-Mare

THE HOUSE

The house was in the middle of an abandoned theme park. It was spooky, no one around. Small animals rummaged in the dustbins. I'd heard stories that you should never go in there at night. I walked in. It was dark, grey, death all around. Suddenly, I heard a smash. Someone was in here with me.

I heard voices, 'Come closer,' they said. 'We want to play.' It sounded like two little girls. 'Come upstairs.'

I was scared. I tried to run out. The door was locked. 'I'm trapped, I am dead!' I screamed.

SAMUEL OLIVER JACKSON (13)
Worle Community School, Weston-Super-Mare

MY DEAD MOTHER

There I was. My heart pumping out my chest. Terror in my blood. My mother must be under that grave. She's dead! Recently, I keep seeing my mum. It's like she's getting revenge on me for not listening to her and obeying her trust. But science says it's impossible for the dead to come back, but religion doesn't...

I go back to the graveyard at 10pm, so the dead will awake. It starts raining but that doesn't matter as I love the rain. As soon as I say, 'Mother,' she is there behind me, like she knows...

LARA FATTAH (13)
Worle Community School, Weston-Super-Mare

THE EMPIRE

The throne room was cold and unnerving. Everything gathered dust. The chair looked like it hadn't been sat on for ages. It was like the souls of the shattered empire still roamed around regularly. At least it felt like it. The elevator door hadn't moved ever by the looks of it. The emperor's presence was there, like a spider in the centre of his web. Suddenly, the door opened, nobody was there. Ghosts controlled it now. The stairs were stone-dead and the windows were fogged-up. The empire had fallen, but it still lived after after its final demise.

AUSTEN DRISCOLL (14)
Worle Community School, Weston-Super-Mare

FREAK FACE

It was a cold stormy night. Loud thunder claps rumbled through the windows. A strange tapping noise repeated quietly under the wind and rain. I walked to the window. A sudden flash of lightning revealed a terrifying horror. It was a vampire. Its bloody face was pressed up against the glass. I threw myself into my bed but the sight couldn't leave my mind. Fear drove me downstairs. I hid in the corner, but there was a small gap in the curtains. I sprinted over and closed them. Suddenly, I felt two fangs dig into my neck. I screamed.

HARRY REYNOLDS (14)
Worle Community School, Weston-Super-Mare

THE DEAD GIRL

Silence followed me wherever I turned, broken occasionally by crows screeching or twigs snapping. The moon lit up this building in front of me. Blood dripped down the walls. I wanted to run, but my heart wouldn't let me. Suddenly, I felt myself being dragged down these steps and locked in this confined room. My heart raced. *Bang!* Something hit the door hard. My heart was now pounding and was beating out of my chest! I could hear something mumbling behind me. As I turned around, my eyes getting used to darkness, I saw the figure of a young girl...

SOPHIE BEAUCHEMIN (14)
Worle Community School, Weston-Super-Mare

WHEN NIGHTMARES COME TRUE

Most people can wake from nightmares knowing they aren't true. It's different for me. My nightmares came true and were slowly killing me. Until one really did.
Waking up in a white room, I searched for a way out. Anger hit as there wasn't a way out! I screamed but no noise came out. Suddenly, I felt like I was being dragged. Sharp pain smothered me as I tried to pull away. I never remembered anything after that. I no longer had feelings. Opening my eyes was impossible. I felt dead because the truth is, I was...

OLIVIA BRUNT (13)
Worle Community School, Weston-Super-Mare

THE BROKEN CHURCH

Around the broken church lay hundreds of graves each with a single flower on the freshly dug dirt. I shivered. The cold made me go inside the church where the lamp swung and the seats creaked. Was someone there? I called out, and the coffin at the end of the room rocked. *Bang! Bang!* Then it came. The skeleton sat up with a jolt and stared deeply into my soul. I knew this was bad so I ran but the door slammed shut. I could hear the clanking of the bones as the skeleton rose from its coffin. 'Help me!'

GEMMA CARNELL (13)
Worle Community School, Weston-Super-Mare

TONGUES

She was bullied. Physical. Verbal. Cyber. Why? Because she was mute. A defect from birth. But her bullies never realised what she was capable of with a sharpened blade. She had gone on a rampage whilst they slept. Silencing their harsh words... In her house there was a dim hallway with peeling plaster. A hallway filled with intricately designed, gold-cased frames. Frames filled with tongues. Limp, lifeless and dried up. Hundreds of them, pinned to their boards. People's cut-out tongues. Not just her bullies, though... If she couldn't talk, why should they?

MEG SNOOK (14)
Worle Community School, Weston-Super-Mare

PETE!

Last night something traumatic happened. So here it goes... I walked down to the graveyard with my friend Jess. We lost Pete four months ago due to cancer. Anyway, as we made our way down to Pete's grave, we hard a rustle in the bushes next to us. Jess got scared and I told her that it was just a hedgehog or something. We then carried on towards the bottom of the graveyard. Suddenly, I got the feeling we were being followed. I turned around and there, standing covered in dirt, was... Pete...

DIONNÉ MEINTJES (14)
Worle Community School, Weston-Super-Mare

IS IT YOU?

There was a sixteen-year-old called Dean. He lived with his mum and three sisters. He'd recently discovered his great-grandad had died in his house due to a heart attack. Dean set out on a mission to go to his old house.
When he got there (at 11 o'clock at night) he heard noises from every direction. A deadly scream disturbed the silence. The trees danced as Dean entered the mysterious house. He saw a rat scurrying across the damp floorboards. Suddenly, Dean caught a glimpse of a transparent figure. Could this be Dean's long-lost great-grandad?

GRACE LINDFIELD (13)
Worle Community School, Weston-Super-Mare

THE EVIL PRESENCE

Ouch! I hit the floor. In pain, I shouted for my friend... 'Aiden!'
'I'm here!'
I ran towards him and we both wondered where we were. The room
was so echoey, cold and felt so large. We saw a shadow getting
closer. I felt a hand on my shoulder. An evil presence was behind
me. We screamed and I hit it in the mouth. We ran and it ran into a
wall. The end! We managed to escape to the the outside fresh air.
That house was evil. We were in the car. Another hand laid on my
shoulder...

NATALIA TRIPP (14)
Worle Community School, Weston-Super-Mare

Z-DAY

This day seemed completely different from usual. The streets were
dead. Cars with no windows and a scream every hour. I investigated
the street with a bat by my side to protect me from whatever was out
there. A groan came from behind me whilst I felt a breath of that thing
shiver down my neck. I turned and it was a zombie! Is this really what
was going on? I hopped in my van and drove to the local store. I
walked in armed and ready for what was going to happen. The lights
flickered. I got bitten.

JAKE WHITE (13)
Worle Community School, Weston-Super-Mare

THE CLOCK FROZE

The clock froze. The small Tudor village was once silent with only the whispers of the wind and the creaking of doors that could be heard. Now it was a horrific bloodbath of hatred. Brothers turned on sisters, friend on friend. The thought of love didn't live here anymore, just the believing of dictatorship; only power filled their hearts. Corpses wove the streets like a blanket of blood. A small boy stared out of the clock window, a grin flooded his sunken face. The *tick-tock* of the clock now echoed the no longer living streets of eternal death.

BEKAH WHITFIELD (13)
Worle Community School, Weston-Super-Mare

CREATION 2.0

The beast awoke from its deep slumber! I violently shivered with fear and excitement, knocking over several lab bottles as a result. The monster's bleary scarlet eyes swivelled around the room as it made low mumbles of incoherent noise. I looked contently as its tight skin managed to cover the atrocities that lay beneath. The monster soon became restless and began to fidget in the restraint it was trapped in. Creation 2.0 (as the beast was now named) suddenly made a piercing shriek and broke away from the table it was tied to. A wave of panic washed over me...

EMILY WEAVER (14)
Worle Community School, Weston-Super-Mare

DOWN

The mud was thick, I was slowly sinking. I felt a little tickle on my back and then a tremendous amount of pain. I yelped, squirming around in the mud trying to free my hands. I managed to get one loose but I was bitten. I was paralysed, everything went fuzzy then dark. My arms were rotten, green and mushy. I heard my skin sizzling. My bones were cracking. I murmured, 'Help.' I knew no one would come out to give me hope. The mud had risen over my face. I was prepared for death.

KURT NEAL (13)
Worle Community School, Weston-Super-Mare

LIVING WITH ASPERGERS

'Ha, ha, ha!' The lecherous laugh deafened my ears. I curled up in a ball rocking back and forth wishing for it to stop. 'It's only a dream,' I repeatedly whispered to myself. The noise grew louder within seconds. My worst fear was alive - it was here, with me. My mum rushed in as she heard me screaming. I started to hear other spiritual noises. They filled my brain making me crazy, confused. I got up and started punching the hollow wall. I did complicated calculations in my head to try and focus. Seeing a clown, my mind shut down.

ELANA TITCOMBE (14)
Worle Community School, Weston-Super-Mare

Uncle Tim

I woke up to see the ghostly figure of my Uncle Tim. He was whimpering something, but all I could hear was gibberish. I had no idea what to do. I tried to communicate with him but every time I tried to speak to him he would just scream like a newborn baby. He started to get closer and closer. My body temperature started to drop. I was a frozen fish. He touched me and I could hear everything he could. He finally replied to me with... 'You left the gas on... ' and then he suddenly flashed away forever...

JACOB CHRISTIAN PANG (13)
Worle Community School, Weston-Super-Mare

The Touch

The asylum door creaks as footsteps echo, giggling is heard. The room is cold and broken. Two men step in. 'It is quite chilly in here,' says Robert grasping his knife. His brother James nods and pulls out his canteen.
Suddenly, a small figure appears. It is a girl she asks, 'Where's my mummy?' She repeats it each time more demonic.
Robert approaches the girl and grabs her shoulder while reassuring her. A large screech as loud as a car's wheels. She disappears.
Robert's eyes turn red and Robert throws his knife. He smiles, then commits suicide.
'Goodbye,' she says.

LUKE HARRISON DAVIES (13)
Worle Community School, Weston-Super-Mare

RUNAWAY BRIDE

As she walks down the street with her head looking towards the ground, people are curious. Has she come from a funeral looking sad? But no, she is on her way to her wedding. She finally arrives at the bright church. She instantly dampens the mood. The long ceremony is over. She is dreading the after party since she is as unsociable as a teenager on their phone! Finally the party's over. On their way up to their room she strikes; she takes the knife out of her veil and she leaves him in a puddle of blood...

OLIVIA RUSSE (13)
Worle Community School, Weston-Super-Mare

THE BEAST INSIDE

As the light of the full moon hit my skin I started to change. The transformation from human to beast. I was slowly turning. Turning into the beast inside. I was growing fur everywhere... everywhere, claws ripped through the skin of my hands and feet; my hair was getting thicker and longer until it was like a mane. My nose turned into a snout and my ears grew big and pointed, and my hands and feet into powerful paws. Throughout the transformation I could feel the darkness slowly consuming me and taking control of my body. The beast had awoken.

TOM BIGGS (13)
Worle Community School, Weston-Super-Mare

Bride Of Dracula?

I stood outside the house; the sombre clouds darkened my mood. I walked in the house and into the dark living room which had a flickering bulb. Every time the light twitched I swore I saw a darkened outline of someone in the corner. It walked towards me. The long drape of its pitch-black dress dragging behind - and that's when I realised it was a woman. It was Draculaess. Her fangs were pearl-white and razor-sharp. She swiftly moved towards me, opening her mouth. But I backed away quickly. She fiercely bit my neck, blood dripped, that was it!

SHANNON HORN (13)
Worle Community School, Weston-Super-Mare

The Demon

As I nervously walk through a gloomy, abandoned town, I stumble across an old, broken building. I look around the dimly lit house. I spot a mysterious door, slightly open. Creeping towards it carefully, I pause, suddenly I get violently jerked back and I'm being pulled by someone or something down some stairs. Landing on the cold, hard ground, I'm disorientated. Lying there, screaming, the dark figure in the corner stares back at me, with his red eyes filled with manic fury. I can't move. The demon rushes towards me. Looking into its eyes, I take my last breath.

MOLLY BURTON-DICKIE (13)
Worle Community School, Weston-Super-Mare

THE HAUNTED CHURCH

He crept down the church's eerie hallway, unsure if anyone was watching him. He suddenly felt his legs go numb, which petrified him. As he lay, still as a statue, a cackling sound was made behind him. He looked up to see a translucent figure. Its teeth were whiter than snow and its eyes were daggers. He reached up to punch the entity away, but it floated above him. There was a smash on the window, which startled the figure. It flew out of the now open window. He then crawled out of the church to comprehend what had happened.

FINLEY DOWLING (13)
Worle Community School, Weston-Super-Mare

SLIPPING SANITY

'It all started on Halloween night. I was taking my younger sister trick or treating until a costumed figure emerged from the shadows. She sprinted towards the twisted trees. I had nearly caught up when I crashed towards the leaf-littered ground. The air was knocked out of my lungs as I was pinned down. The giant creature's powerful jaws locked around my throat. Its slimy saliva fused with my crimson blood. My bones began to crack and contort into a different form. I became the being that haunts my dreams.'
'He is crazy,' the judge stated. 'To the mad house!'

FAITH TREW (14)
Worle Community School, Weston-Super-Mare

Brother Turns On Brother

The brother dropped down dead. Damon smiled at the sight. He removed the stake from the frozen body. 'I will never let them live Elijah!'
'They don't deserve to die!'
The brothers looked at the pile of rotting men and women. They looked like a dump. The moon shone through the boarding house's windows showing the weird woods; the beasts that lay inside. The house that was as old as space stood ready to fall. The look on Damon's face was stormy. It went with the weather. With a stake in hand, he stabbed his brother. He dropped down dead.

Alaina Hodge (13)
Worle Community School, Weston-Super-Mare

The Master's Dungeon

He was explaining how the master of the castle had been mercilessly tortured by his servants in the room they were now standing in. Ben's ears pricked up at this.
As the tour guide said this, a low moan issued from the corner. Someone started to sing, 'I own the castle, I own the dungeon and now I own your soul!' The chains on the wall started to clash together menacingly. The barred door clanged shut. Torture devices rattled in anticipation. Ben's legs shook in fear.
'I own the castle, I own the dungeon and now I own your soul!'

Matt Southcombe (13)
Worle Community School, Weston-Super-Mare

REMEMBERING

Two years ago my whole family died a tragic death. I don't remember, but I'm the only survivor. Now it's time to know the truth! I inject myself with serum, now I'm inside my own head... there it is, my memory! I watch my mind show me what happened.
I was at home with my family, it was Christmas. A tall, broad man appeared at the door. We ignored it! He kept knocking so we answered. I screamed as he threw a large flame into the house. Without realising it, I was the only one who made it out alive.

LOUISE CHAPMAN (13)
Worle Community School, Weston-Super-Mare

SHAKESPEARED

A couple were watching Romeo and Juliet at the top of the theatre. The wood under them was rotting and collapsed, causing them to fall to their deaths. Now two teens have decided to wander the theatre.
'Hey Jerry, can we get out of here?'
'No Homer! Not until we see some dead bodies.'
'But what if this place is haunted?'
'If it's haunted, then I will buy you a pizza.'
Scream!
Jerry ran towards it and something cold and gentle stroked his face. Jerry dropped dead. Darkness slowly grasped Homer, engulfing, absorbing him.
'Homer is mine... '

JACK BAILEY (14)
Worle Community School, Weston-Super-Mare

Taken

We were lost in the deep, dark woods. It was pouring down with rain and it was pitch-black. But suddenly we stumbled across a huge cemetery. It was so, so huge that we couldn't even see the end. We started to walk through to see if we knew where we were. Out of nowhere, someone chucked a sack over us and we were carried away. When we were put down, a car engine started and we left in it. When they took the sacks off our heads we saw thousands of dead bodies all in one room...

RYAN LATHAM (13)
Worle Community School, Weston-Super-Mare

The Graveyard

We were strolling towards the graveyard. We were both very anxious about two things: the body in the grave and whether the treasure would be in there. We gathered our thoughts and equipment and started digging frantically. As we got deeper into the grave we started to see the old, cracked, dirty bones, but we kept digging. We reached the full bottom of the grave. There was a treasure chest. Our hearts filled with joy! We opened the chest. We found the most mysterious thing; it was ugly, but cute. It was cold, but hot. It was a...

SCOTT TIMBERLAKE (14)
Worle Community School, Weston-Super-Mare

THE WHISPER

The trees all around looked the same. The night made it hard to see. She started to sprint. She was panting as she ran. She landed on a twig, which startled the birds. Ravens squawked at the sight of her. An outstretched branch smacked her in the face, which knocked her over. She got up and looked around. She heard something move behind her. She held her breath. She grasped the necklace around her neck. It had a Christian cross on it. She heard a whisper behind her, 'Don't run, you're just wasting time!' She spun around. Nothing was there.

LIAM TICKTUM (13)
Worle Community School, Weston-Super-Mare

THE CAR CRASH

I ran out of the church screaming. I opened my car door, got into the car and sped off. Suddenly, out of nowhere, the car drove itself into a tree. I woke up standing on the edge of a cliff with the three babies that were in the church. One of the kids grabbed my hand and then *smack,* onto the rocks, the sea then pulling me, down to the bottom. All I was thinking was, *where are the kids?* I looked up and there were the kids with their mother and father looking down at me laughing. I died.

ERIN FRANCIS (13)
Worle Community School, Weston-Super-Mare

Est.1991

YOUNG WRITERS
INFORMATION

We hope you have enjoyed reading this book – and
that you will continue to in the coming years.

If you're a young writer who enjoys reading and creative writing, or the
parent of an enthusiastic poet or story writer, do visit our website
www.youngwriters.co.uk. Here you will find free
competitions, workshops and games, as well as
recommended reads, a poetry glossary and our blog.

If you would like to order further copies of this book, or any of our other
titles, then please give us a call or visit **www.youngwriters.co.uk**.

Young Writers
Remus House
Coltsfoot Drive
Peterborough
PE2 9BF
(01733) 890066 / 898110
info@youngwriters.co.uk